The Girl Down Cellar

A Novel by

Marlene Walker

Special Thanks to:

Nancy LaRonda Johnson
Dr. Judith Linzer
Sally Thomas
Sherri Hedman
Andrea Beach
Kevin Knarr
Duncan Knarr
Margaret Senneff
Lia DeLand
Hayward Public Library Peer Writers

ISBN: 978-0-9903108-0-8

*Why'd you go
Down Cellar?
Why'd you brave the cold?*

*I'd things to do
Down Cellar.
'Mid the dust and mold.*

Kory Stamp

Contents

Prelude

Long before you were born there lived a princess called Danae. Sounds ideal, right? Every little girl wants to grow up to be a royal daughter, with the fluffy pink dress, the shiny tiara and the magic wand. Ah, but that's a *fairy* princess, which Danae was not. Although, she probably wished she were, as her story unfolded; a magic wand would have come in handy then.

What happened was, when Danae was teetering on the brink of womanhood, the local soothsayer told her father, the King of Argos, that he would one day be killed by his grandson.

"I don't even have a grandson, fool," laughed the king.

"Not yet," winked the soothsayer.

The king laughed in his face: "My daughter, a mother? Ridiculous. She's still my little girl."

Just then Danae walked by, her womanliness straining her girlish gown at the seams, and the implications of the soothsayer's words surged through the king: as his sole offspring, Danae was the only one who could give him a homicidal grandson.

"Build me a little house!" he bellowed to the Royal Carpenter. "Let it have walls of stone and a bronze roof with a tiny skylight through which meals and water may be lowered."

"Where shall I build it, King?" asked the Royal Carpenter.

"Underground, enclosed with thick earthen walls no mortal man could penetrate."

As is widely known, Zeus infused his seed through the skylight, and thereby, in one of the lesser known instances of virgin conception, impregnated the innocent Danae, who knew nothing of what happened to her.

Some months later the sound of a baby's cry was heard coming from Danae's cell. Without a second's hesitation, the king had mother and child tossed into the sea.

But karma was not invented yesterday: Danae's son, Perseus, was rescued, and grew up to kill his grandfather unknowingly in a gladiatorial contest. Not much nuance to reexamine in the mentality of either the self-absorbed grandfather or the cutthroat grandson.

But why does the myth not tell how the cruelty and betrayal of Danae's father impacted her mind? What did she feel, banned from her father's presence and imprisoned underground without her mother's embrace? How did she survive without the touch of a breeze, or the feel of grass under her feet? And did she even know what was happening to her as her body ballooned out of shape and then something very large began to push its way out of her? How did she deal with her horror, her incredible pain? And, most importantly, did she go mad. Or did she somehow manage to preserve her sanity? Was she thus transformed from a passive victim to an active advocate for her own well-being?

Alas, the myth-makers did not delve into Danae's psyche. They left it to us to do that.

A View of the Silky

Lowering myself to my stone front steps, I was overwhelmed by the thought that, for the next nine days, I would taste freedom for the first time in years. My husband, Larry, was going fishing and my parents were taking our five-year old boy to the beach with them for a whole week. During the nine days my husband was granting me, I would be able to start painting again. No other inducement could have convinced me to let my mother and father pick up Bertie the day before and take him on vacation with them to Long Beach, Washington. As Bertie had never been away from me more than overnight, I would miss him horribly. But I was as excited about having the time alone to paint as Bertie was to go clam digging with his gramma and grandpa. I sipped my jasmine tea, grasping the cup firmly to calm the jitters of anticipation. Thoughts of the days ahead alone with my easel and paints made my hands shake so violently the jasmine blossoms quivered.

My first year at home in a decade and the weather had been a painter's dream. Last fall the trees turned color with flashes of drama, and in my mind I had completed piles of paintings--dreamlike leaves of impossible colors. In winter, I planned the snowy brush strokes of a silver thaw; in spring, I saw local wild flowers papering my walls; and, this morning, catching sight of the vibrant sweep of August colors stretching from my house to the river was like being slapped in the face with a Van Gogh. Summer grasses roiled in a hot wind, the ancient apple trees downslope from the house waved their scaly arms in a wicked dance, the rapids beyond the meadow swept snowdrifts of cottonwood fluff down towards the Columbia, and a boiling vapor rose as the sun struck the dewy lawn. Earth sighed in the throes of passion. It was not a typical Oregon day.

I cannot look at this landscape in any weather without envisioning it as a painting, but on such a beautiful, cloudless Oregon morning, my mind always

3

unleashes visions whose colors extend beyond three dimensions. Passing by the front window at dawn, I had watched the sun come over Mt. Hood on a coppery bright wave. Now, I let my gaze float downhill where the golden meadow grass spread its velvet cape below the porch. The new sun framed the landscape on the opposite bank of the river with a sensual metallic aura. In such a sunrise, I imagined I saw mythical creatures of wind, sea, earth, and air performing magical rescues and other long neglected acts of justice.

I almost called my husband to come look at the sight. The libidinous colors of an August sunrise always reminded me of the first morning I awoke with Larry's head on the pillow beside mine, his face as sweet as a young Buddha's. The skin of his forehead had the invisible down and the powdery smell of a baby's. The sun, just reaching its first slender crescent of light over the low windowsill, had set the blond hair on his naked silhouette afire, and I imagined he was my own Greek God, forever. I knew his body was not as muscular or classically proportioned as, say, Achilles', but, when he felt me looking at him and woke, reached an arm up around my neck and pulled me down to him, murmuring, *Oh, Kory, Kory!*, I thought he would always be the god of love to me.

My best friend, Teresa, had asked how such an affectionate person as myself could go for a boy who had *that Boston reserve*. He's not from Boston, I said. *Kory, I think his gonads may be from Siberia,* Teresa answered. He's not so good in a crowd, I told her, but as the song says, when you get him alone, you'd be surprised. And, I had been right. The night before, Larry and I had been two nervous virgins, but that morning, making love in the sunrise, we were lovers complete.

Contemplating things on the steps years later, I did not know why we had not made love by the light of a sunrise in so long. Heaven knows I had tried to entice him. Maybe if I called him to see *this* sunrise, he would pull me to him and make love to me on the carpet or the couch, or the porch swing; I would not say no if he rolled me around on the cold stone steps. I did not call him, though. My experiences with such enticements of late told me he would only have kidded me for what he called my unduly fanciful side. After the glow of courtship and the honeymoon weeks had worn off, Larry had refused even to cast an eye on a common sunset, reserving his regard for the truly spectacular ones. I had learned not to let the poetry and images I savored or my admiration for common sunsets seep out in everyday conversation, but I could not shut them out of my head. So vividly did that view of the sunrise strike me that, just thinking of painting the sundrenched bank of the Silky River made me breathless. I still had two passions, Larry and painting, but sadly neither of them were at my fingertips anymore.

All the more reason for the thrill I felt every time I remembered that I would soon resume painting--though not for the eyes of my nearest and dearest. For my private parlor, I painted my favorite mythical motifs cryptically, blending figures of gods and goddesses, totems and heroes into the lines of my home landscape, tucking figures from mythology into each painting: a Native American coyote scuttling across the scene with mischief on her mind– the color and texture of her coat blending into the dry meadow grasses. That was how I used to discharge my dreams and fears without calling attention to them. I did not think I could stand to have one more painting session interrupted by a doubting Thomas in my family; therefore, I would let my *unduly fanciful* artistic visions of my front yard go until Larry had gone fishing.

Still, with brush-stroke glances, I took in the scene from the porch one more time before preparing the household for my nine-day furlough from married life, when I would paint large the imps of my mind for my gallery show.

Without telling Larry, I had entered some of my visions of the indigenous myths of the Columbia River

Basin at the Sacagawea County Fair earlier in the month and won a prize. Better than that, I had received a request from a Riverport gallery owner to show my entire collection of paintings in late fall. It would be my first showing on the west coast since receiving my Master of Fine Arts degree. Larry looked embarrassed when I told him, but I felt a thrill when I thought of how I would lay all my work out on the living and dining room floors after he had gone--with what pleasure I would arrange sketches, watercolors, charcoals, crayon, and chalk paintings until I had them in the order I wanted to hang them for my show. And then I would paint new pictures. How I would paint.

To control my excitement, I closed my eyes and listened. The world seemed less urgent than when I stared openly at the vital scene surrounding my home. Soon I began to feel the day humming in self-content around me. The bees were busy in the purple clover, grasshoppers whirred through the pollen-filled air, and swarms of nasty yellow jackets continued their seasonal orgy among the windfall apples in the orchard. On such a day, I had to admit that, despite the tension that had increased between Larry and me since we returned from school on the east coast, it was gratifying to be living in the family home again.

Sitting on the steps where I had played as a little girl, listening to the song of summer, I wished it could heal all that was strained in my life. In all the years I had been living in the cramped apartments where Larry and I spent our dark graduate school days struggling with college, with marriage, with raising our young son, I had always imagined myself sitting on the steps of this porch sweeping the river scene with half-closed eyes. At that time, I had believed returning to the family place on the river could heal whatever had been reviving the childhood nightmare that still clung. But, last night I had been so excited about Larry's imminent departure and having a week to myself to paint for my upcoming show that I had slept lightly and lurched awake from my chronic nightmare--the monster lurking in the riverbank at the foot of the orchard ready to ambush me with a chilling roar.

Whatever my dream monster signified, it had come very close the night before and peered right into my face. It is always nearly invisible and its coat so dark it shines turquoise in the moonlight, its face pale like a human mask. But it spoke with a familiar voice.

With a gasp, I recalled waking with its image still pasted on my lenses-- its eyes glittering through slits in the dream mask.

Who are you?

"I am your husband, and I am trying to sleep," Larry had grumbled last night. When he spoke, the image of the eyes and mask dissolved, its atoms dispersing themselves among the dust motes in our bedroom.

"Sorry," I murmured, "I'll try to sleep quieter next time."

I sighed over the lip of my tea mug and a jasmine blossom went skating across the cup like a white-sailed fairy ship.

"Take my fears with you," I whispered.

Not time to think about the nightmare yet. Later, when I unfold my easel and take my brush in hand. I tremble with the image which is moving from mind to fingertips. So many mornings like this one I had rushed to the sunroom, eager to work. The brush always flowing towards the waiting paper. But, the first stroke never falls. A child awakens, a husband returns early from work, a mother calls, and calls, and calls until the paint, paper, palette and easel are put away until another day when the artist will own her own hours. One day, I failed to move to the sun porch, to unfurl the easel or squeeze paint onto the palette. I feel familial love separating me from my core, as Mother Earth is separated from the sky by a silver thaw. I open my eyes as if to see if my feeling is mirrored by the stifling loveliness of a silver thaw. *No, it is summer and I am home.*

Looking downslope at the Silky River from my porch that morning, I felt a sudden wave of gratitude towards my mother and father. Though my parents exemplified most of the clumsiness of the Great Depression School of Parenting, I reminded myself how glad I was that my folks had made me the beneficiary of their relocation. Absurdly fearful in their advancing years of living five minutes farther from Salmon Run's only hospital, they had moved two miles closer to civilization down River Road. And, thanks to their fears, now that I was home again and able to gaze at this splendorous view every day, I would find a way to paint again.

I gulped some tea and closed my eyes, listening to the Silky's eager progress towards the Columbia. Mid-sigh my breath caught. Something was missing in the morning. I looked for it in the meadow but did not find it. Closed my eyes and listened for it in the orchard, but did not hear it. Listened for it in the river's voice, and only then recalled the missing notes of the morning song: the laughter of a Native American family, mother and five children, who used to bathe every day in the shallows across the river. Sometimes a few miniature marauding braves would even swim across the river and pick fruit from our aging orchard. I wondered if the children whose hushed laughter I had heard across the river a few times this summer were remnants of that family who once lived in the abandoned construction cabin east of the railroad bridge. I wondered if they knew of the disaster that had occurred years before, when I was an undergraduate home on vacation. I listened for the sounds of their trespassing, but did not hear their muffled voices. Without them, the August day turned empty and stagnant. I still carried in my mind the idyllic picture of those *wild Indians*--as my mother had called them-- and the terrifying event that disturbed the untroubled days when they used to summer across the river.

Sitting on my front porch, on the brink of my moment of freedom, I let my mind go back to a time when I was a child and would eavesdrop on the Native American children swimming, playing, and listening to their mother's stories.   I smiled in anticipation of painting them as soon as Larry left. Dozens of times I had reproduced my view of that native family, and I never tired of looking at those pictures. Wherever I went, I carried my portfolio: stacks of pastels and charcoal sketches of pictures of those children enacting their mother's tales. Painting this childhood scene had buoyed me up while I was living in the nature-starved eastern cities of my university and gallery years. Those paintings were part of me; my journal and my charm against despair.

Usually the children stayed on the eastern side of the river, sun bathing on the boulders across from our orchard or diving off of them while their laughing mother watched from a woven blanket spread on the sand. She sat cross-legged with her ochre, gold, teal, and deep blue skirt forming a hammock of her lap where first one child and then another-- sometimes three or more at one time-- would tumble, laughing up into her round face. Sometimes, on a narrow sand spit, the mother would kneel over the water to bathe the younger ones. Cottonwood branches were the clotheslines where the mother hung her morning laundry.

I would run down the lane every morning of my childhood (when it was not raining) and--using the excuse of picking currants, raspberries, blackcaps or gooseberries from the rows of vines that ran along the side of the lane opposite the orchard--I would eavesdrop on the family. Autumn was the best time to watch them from a grassy tunnel I made with my body under a monster blackberry vine that ran down to the river on the orchard side at the bottom of our lane. From my vantage point, I could not see the near bank but I could see the children playing or listening to stories on the opposite shore. Unaware of the scratches the vines were making

9

on my arms and legs when I was wriggling in under the blackberries, I felt a hunger no one but another only child could understand. I would think, if I could wish for one thing in life I did not have, it would be a lap like that to comfort me and someone who took time to tell me stories on a sunny afternoon. My son Bertie had access to such a lap--I made sure of that--but I could not remember my mother ever providing one. And, I was certain my husband's mother had offered no such welcoming nest.

Perhaps it was the dramatic circumstance of eavesdropping that made the stories so memorable for me, but often when I am in a crisis situation, one of those legends will pop into my head, and always with good reason. My lifelong fascination with myths as they impinge on daily life was born of that native mother's tales. Only in college did I learn my own ancestral myths, yet I still felt closer to the stories of the Native Americans of the Columbia River basin. Those tales were my best friends and snuggest comfort when anything disturbing happened in my life. I was not surprised, therefore, to be thinking about them now.

When the native family picked up their woven blankets, left the river and went home for the day, an oft unacknowledged sadness up-surged in my ostensibly cheerful life. The loss of their company would have crushed me if I had not found compensatory remedies in play. After they had wrapped their blankets around themselves and melted into the cottonwood scrub, I would slide backwards out of my hiding place and fashion a headband of braided grain, make a tomahawk by tying a stone to a broken branch, paint my face with berry juice, fashion flower bracelets for my wrists and a loincloth of giant rhubarb leaves. Garbed as I imagined my secret playmates dressed when they were on their home turf, I would act out the stories the mother had told on the riverbank. In my early years, I imitated every Native American custom I thought my unsuspecting playmates followed in the privacy of their own railroad shack.

I would run around the field between our house and the river, chopping off cavalry members' heads and doing war dances until my mother would call me in and scold me for acting like a *wild Indian.* She said it to humiliate me into acting like a lady, but I took secret pleasure in the epithet. That the "wild Indians'" mothers took them swimming every day, below the orchard, where I was forbidden to go only enhanced their bravery, their independence and their romantic way of life to me. And, when my mother would call me home to supper, I would reply with a blood-curdling war cry.

"I'm surprised a *wild Indian* like yourself doesn't eat with her fingers," said my mother once at dinner. I dropped my fork and began eating as she had suggested, and she never said that again. After that I noticed my mother seemed able to sense that family's presence whenever they came swimming or fishing or apple picking along the river banks. Before long, I would feel her eyes on my back as I snuck down to my listening post under the blackberry vines. Then one day, when I had been listening to the native woman tell a story, and I was watching her boys swim toward our side of the river with the intention to pick up apples, I heard my mama running down the lane from the house, crying, *Scamps!* Back then she protected her property the way her hens defended their eggs from me when I tried to gather them from beneath their warm, feathery bosoms. I did not stay to see the Native American family scatter into the brush on the far bank. This terrified wild Indian ran to the back of the house and hid behind the "Kissing Boulders," two gigantic rocks at the foot of the bluff in our back yard. I never told my mother when I saw the *wild Indians* swim to our side of the river, but she managed to humiliate me every time they tried, as she scurried down the lane towards the lower orchard flapping her seersucker apron at unseen culprits, shouting *Scat, you scamps!* Despite my growing familiarity with those children, I thought *scamp* was an ugly curse word,

11

and associated it with the monster my mother had suggested dwelt along that stretch of the river.

Now, I ran my eye over the tops of the orchard trees. From the porch they looked wholesome and robust, their leaves turning gold as doubloons in the autumn sun. Whenever I ran down the lane to the Silky, however, I had seen that the trunks were twisted and black with mossy grey scale peeling off of them, and piles of the fruit lay rotting with a sickly sweet stench in drifts of tarry leaves in the dense shade of the branches. As that old orchard led to the riverbank site of those bad childhood dreams, I wondered why as new owners, Larry and I had not made certain that the diseased trees were bulldozed into oblivion when my parents handed me the deed to their home. Maybe because the autumnal woodland balanced the scene so well, to the painter's eye? Maybe because I associated the monster on our river bank with the figures in native myths I loved to paint? My memories of the little braves had already sparked one painting I planned to complete in the coming days. Watching those boys leap about in my mind, I began to see how to integrate their mother's stories into my paintings of the landscape I loved--as soon as Larry was gone.

The stone steps were cooling my rear end, as I began–mentally--to choose the paints and brushes I would need to begin my nine-day binge. Over the years, to lift my consciousness above the mundane circumstances that weighed me down from time to time, I had developed my own form of artistic fantasizing I called "mind-painting," in which I closed my eyes and visualized what I wanted to paint. The method raised me above the demands of my mother's incessant phone calls, my father's requests for lengthy coffee breaks, and Larry's requirement that I stand outside the bathroom door while he read to me from the Sunday paper. After years of practice, I could even mind-paint with my eyes open. I would nod and murmur occasionally at my family members' comments, while all the time I would be planning a painting.

As I felt the sun touch my knees, I ran my memory of the day of my first silver thaw through my mind and began to sketch figures into an air painting with my fingertip. The easel unfolds, its joints creaking like the bones of a crone rising from her winter bed. The brush comes to my palm like the comforting hand of a well-worn friend. I tremble with the image which is moving from mind to fingertips. The brush flows towards the waiting paper where I see me soaring high on the swing Daddy hung for me on a tree branch, the swing ropes shedding icicles which catch the sunlight make exclamation points of light shoot out all around me. A thick glaze of frozen water encases every surface making our house and yard look like a fairyland of crystal rock candy. My bones are encased in ice. I am four.

Larry discovered me, sitting on the front porch in my robe, finger painting with imaginary colors. He had been about to leave to do some last minute shopping for his trip when he interrupted my mind-painting to ask if I had washed the long wool socks he wore under his hip boots. But first, he could not resist commenting on what must have been the ridiculous sight of me daubing my fingers in the air as though painting the sky.

"I see what you are doing," he said.

Larry disapproved of my showing my paintings in public. In a romantic moment, I had divulged to him that the political theme of my paintings, the paradox of ownership of the land; how the Native Americans were part of it before my European ancestors wrenched them from it, yet, beneath that conflict, the land has always been there to nurture all peoples.

"You're indulging in your ethnic sentimentality about the Native American family again. Face it, Kory, they're committing a double crime," he smiled, ever the indulgent owner of a higher SAT score, "They trespass on our property to steal our apples from it."

"Apples we never eat. Besides, my mother never let them get as far as the orchard. Even if she had, don't you think a worthy subject of art would be the paradox of children branded as criminal for trespassing on land we trespassed on first?"

"Land that is now ours, my dear...."

"We didn't buy it from them, Larry. We took it."

"Not you and I, Kory."

"Our ancestors then, or the people who sold the land to our ancestors."

"Possession is nine-tenths of the law, Little Squaw Head-in-the-Clouds."

"But what about the other ten percent?"

"Trust you to worry about the odd lot."

"Let them at least take the odd percent in wormy apples."

"Give 'em an inch, Kory, and they'll take a mile."

"Yeah, like the Indian Nation is about to rise up and take back the Land of the Free from the rest of us." I half-hoped he did not hear me.

"Thought you were going to use the time I'm gone to rest," he said, "And now you're all pumped up about that old squaw and her brood again."

"Painting rests me."

"Fishing rests me. Painting winds you up like a top." A bit of condescension there.

"Separate vacations. Separate restful activities." I shrugged.

"It's not separate vacations!" Larry flared, with drama in his voice. Without turning to look, I felt his face flush a peony red. I concealed a smile. Though Larry could look scary, he was the man I loved, who had cried in my lap after shooting his first forked-horn.

"Fishing is restful," he clucked. "Painting-- especially painting the charming little Indian thieves you're probably imagining painting right now--is too intense for certain people." He placed a button kiss on my head to close my mind, the conversation, and a whole ethnological issue. There it was: a little corral set up for

14

me to keep my emotions in. "At the end of nine days, my creel will be full of food for the larder," Larry said. "What'll your easel be full of?"

"Food for my spiritual larder," I murmured. He could not have heard me: He was already headed into the house. He called over his shoulder, "Pack my bag yet?"

No comment about the black silk kimono I was wearing in place of the cotton nightgown I had slept in last night. Though he and I had not been very cozy since our long-standing disagreements had flamed up like periodic sun spots, I had dug my honeymoon robe out of my hope chest and slipped it on to seduce Larry before he left later in the day on his fishing trip. My attempt at seduction had not been a big success, perhaps because the stink of the scene that had caused the most recent dry spell between us had been too pungent to be overcome by my special-occasion perfume.

When the meadow grass between the house and the river had stood tall and green, Larry and I sat on the porch laughing at the wild rabbits jumping straight up out of the deep grass, as rabbits do in the spring. For a moment I forgot the disagreements that had been harrowing our relationship, until Larry began using his index finger as a gun pretending to shoot the rabbits as if they were in a carnival duck-shoot.

"You wouldn't actually shoot one of the rabbits on our land, would you Larry?" I had asked.

"Oh, no!" he protested, making a manly moue with his lips. "I would only scare them away. Such cute little vermin."

Though he looked pleasant, I had been alarmed that Larry might not be kidding.

"You haven't gotten rid of that shotgun your uncle left you yet? You know I worry about Bertie."

"Keep 'em loaded and teach the kid not to touch 'em. That kept me from Uncle Gregory's guns, and it'll keep Bertie from mine."

"I don't want my son to learn not to touch a gun by shooting off his foot, Larry."

"Have a little faith, Kory!"

Determined not to let his earlier brush-offs or our diverging opinions about guns versus small live creatures ruin our love life, I followed Larry from porch to bedroom, to bathroom, to hall, wafting back and forth in front of him in my slinky black kimono as many times as possible while I was packing his toiletries and clothing, and he was waterproofing his hip boots on the attic stairs. Finally I coyly blocked him from going through the doorway to the bedroom.

"He once called her adorable," Larry kidded, "But now he just calls her a door. Excuse me, may I go into my bedroom, please?"

"I was just looking for an opportunity to give you a loving sendoff," I whispered.

"The only way I want to get off today is to get off on my fishing trip, but I keep being impeded." He slid by me into the bedroom, exclaiming, "Did you remember to pack my wool socks?"

"Who could forget socks I'm required to wash by hand?" I joked.

"My wool Pendleton shirt?"

"You hung it in the back of the closet. Just hand it to me, and I'll pack it."

"It's just a closet, Kory, not a bear's den with an angry bear in it," he chuckled. He pawed his way to the back of his closet, retrieved a green wool plaid shirt and tossed it to me.

"You know I don't like closets," I murmured as I carefully folded his shirt and, with all the care of a mother putting her newborn in its crib, placed it in his duffle.

"I don't like being a weatherman either, but someone's got to support the family," he reminded me.

"The only way you could love being a weatherman more is if you could make it as well as report it," I murmured.

16

"What?"

"It's well you support us," I said. "Thanks."

"Going to the Army Surplus store...extra gear. Leave my bag by the bedroom door. I'll pick it up when I head out for Lake William." He was already headed for his truck.

My amorous advances foiled, I returned to the front porch to fetch the teacup I had left on the top step. Glancing down at the bedraggled jasmine blossoms clinging to the sides of the cup and a tiny puddle of tea grains, I tried to parse the indecipherable message written there.

"Can't tea leaves be only the useless dregs of a drink once in a while?" Larry always teased me. I did have a habit of looking for mystical signs of my destiny in every unusual item or phenomenon I encountered. But I had explained to him that, since art school, no one had encouraged me to do the thing I believed I was cut out to do, and so I looked for affirmation in tea leaves, falling stars and unusual changes in the weather. That is why I had come out onto the porch to soak in some affirmation from nature before beginning my day in earnest. I might see a meaningful cloud shape over the river, spy a new patch of four-leaf clovers, or see a ladybug, a dragonfly or two garter snakes entwined-- a classic sign of rejuvenation. That is what I had heard the Native American mother of the little braves across the river say. And, if I had been born a Navajo, a Wasco, a Multnomah or a Chinook, I would feel right about seeking guidance in Nature, I was sure. I would then have seen my dreams as benevolent guideposts, not as threats.

When I heard the familiar purr of Larry's pick-up motor start behind the house, I leaned against the porch column and watched a ball of dust with his truck inside it disappear north down River Road. Larry would be at the Army Surplus store rooting around for bargains all morning. Time to finish packing his duffel and do my household tasks so I would be ready to start painting the minute Larry returned for his bag and left for Central

17

Oregon. I gave my tea dregs a final swirl and let my eyes probe the broad stretch of land between me and the river one last time for a sign. No ladybug or dragonfly darted across my field of vision.   At that moment, however, something more consequential came into view.

Purposely Not Flirting

I had just risen with the intention of going indoors to begin my housewifely duties when something made me take another look out over the meadow towards the river. Though I knew that piece of land had been farmed before the Second World War, I had been too young when the war broke out to recall what it had looked like under cultivation. It was strange then that often when I painted this scene, I daubed in rows of vegetables on that piece of earth, and a farmer stooping to touch the plants with blunt brown fingers.

Now, as though I had just created him there with mental brush strokes, a man appeared from behind the blackcap row. He walked a few steps into the field by the river and stooped to grab a tuft of meadow grass. Then he shook a clod of earth off its roots. I stood transfixed as though I were in Boston again in mid-winter painting a picture of home and that picture had just come to life. The man squatted near the field's edge, crumbled the clod in his fist and put his hand to his face as if he were smelling the dirt. I was thinking, "Next thing you know he'll be eating it," when the man put a finger to his tongue and, bouncing his fanny slightly on his heels, ruminated on the succulent flavor of the dirt as if it were fine cuisine. "Who would come all the way up river to my private property to eat a handful of dirt?" I wondered. Then the man stood up, and, blushing, I recognized him by the way his overalls pulled taut across his rump.

Nicky Nakamura had been poet laureate of Sacagawea High School and the star quarterback our senior year. My girlfriends and I used to go to the games just to admire the way he moved in those snug football knickers. And, here he was on my property after a dozen years out of high school, looking as good in his denim overalls as he had looked in satin football pants.

Nicky and I had dated only once. When we were sophomores, I asked him to a Sadie Hawkins dance. That evening, I found out that the callouses on Nick's hands were smooth and not lumpy or scratchy like other boys', and that his chest muscles were so well developed that, to be courteous, he danced with his breasts alternating with mine the way women do when they hug. We parked on Devil's Elbow--the local necking spot--but did not fumble around with one another in the car. Nick led me up onto a flat boulder where we could both watch the lights of the fringe of small towns clinging to Riverport's hems. With my hands on the smooth cylinders of muscle bordering his backbone and his hands on the back of my neck, we kissed. I never told anyone how I felt dancing or looking at the nightscape with my chest pressed against Nicky's. My steady, Larry, and I were broken up at the time, but in case we ever reconciled, I did not want my feelings to get back to him. As it was, he pursed his lips whenever I even mentioned the Nakamura name, and I did not want to have to answer to him about my feelings for the star quarterback. Even to Nick, I only spoke facetiously about feelings I had harbored since I was a little girl.

"That was what I would call gentlemanly necking," I told Nick in the car on the way home from our date.

"Because you are a lady," Nick grinned.

"On second thought, I think I will remember it as Nicking," I teased.

"Just so you remember it," he murmured.

After our date, Larry came back to me, Nicky went back to dating cheer leaders, and, after college, married the captain of our high school cheerleading squad, Donna Yoshida. When their little boy was only a baby, Donna was killed on the Nakamura farm. No one would discuss it, and I would never have asked the man, "Say, how was it your wife died anyway?" The farm accident had such an air of mystery about it that none of the gossips who exchanged local legends down at Skippy's General Store and Bait Shop would ever discuss it with me. My mother did tell me that she heard at Skippy's that Nick had been too sad or too busy with his farm and his child since Donna died to get involved with another woman.

On that August day, watching Nicky run his hand through the wild rye in front of my house, I felt a blush permeate me like a new wave on loose sand. My body was reacting as though his fingers were in my wheat-colored hair, as they had been on that date years ago.

Shaking away that deceitful feeling, I realized what Nick was doing on my land. Some days earlier, Larry and I had run into him at Skippy's, and my husband had agreed to let Nick drop by to look at our land with a view to his farming some of it. That had surprised me, but, considering the current state of my love life with Larry, I was not terribly shocked that I had renewed my old habit of fantasizing about Nick. It was a harmless pastime after all, I assured myself, sitting on my front step, imagining running into Farmer Nakamura some day and ending up magically lying together in the meadow, hidden by the tall grass, making love as in a picture of a faraway land. Watching Nick survey the shimmering field of gold below me, I laughed at myself: just a nice married lady who had been wedded too long to poeticize about her husband and not long enough to have unlocked the secret of his heart.

I scraped the last wilted jasmine blossoms clinging to my cup into the flower bed and turned to go inside the house to attack my day.

"Missus!" someone called, and, wrapping my robe tight around my throat, I peered around the north side of the porch. The homeless man Nick hired in season was waving at me from Nick's pickup. "Okay if I pick some of these apples for my lunch, Missus?" His red-rimmed eyes and grizzled beard saddened and repulsed me at once, but I shook my head no. Not that I begrudged him the apples, but I shuddered to think of him showing up again and again to ask for more apples, and then some pears and cherries, which were closer to the house. I was alone all day when Larry was at work and I just thought it unwise. Besides, if I had agreed, Larry would have lectured me for days. I scurried into the house, and slid my siren's robe off my shoulders. When I had married, somebody told me that if I left my sexiest nightgown hanging in the bathroom, my husband would get excited every time he went in there to shower. Though the trick had not worked yet, I hung it on the back of the bathroom door just in case.

When I had finished packing Larry's duffel, I zipped it closed and shifted from a bedroom to a kitchen state of mind. I just had time before Larry returned from shopping to finish picking and canning the batch of red huckleberries that had been ripening on the bluff. I smiled at the thought of surprising Larry with a tray full of freshly canned berries when he came back to pick up his duffle and lunch. "We'll just see who provides more food for the larder," I thought.

Though I believed my true vocation was the fine arts, that morning I would put up every berry on the property before I put one dab of paint on canvas. For no logical reason, I believed completing that task would help free me from the age-old nightmares and marital bickering. Larry would bring home fish for the family to find I had provided jam.

I pulled on some shorts and a tee shirt, wrapped a scarf around my hair and tied it at the nape. Striding through the house and out the kitchen door, I grabbed my buckets from the back porch on the way. I was headed for a stand of red huckleberry bushes growing in the rotting stumps still rooted part way up the bluff in our backyard.

As far as I knew, Nicky and I were the only ones who knew about the path up the steep cliff behind our house that led to the Nakamura farm. Though Nick and I had been estranged for some of our high school years, we had been buddies in grade school when I showed him my secret path up the bluff. For some reason I had never told Larry that Nicky had ever played at my house when we were little, that there were red huckleberries in our back yard, or that I was planning to climb a dozen feet up a hidden switchback trail to fetch some for jelly. Larry contended there was no such thing as a red huckleberry. "Only unripe ones," he would smile indulgently at me. I had done some library research and had shown the results to him, but he had pursed his lips and refused to discuss the subject further. Eventually, I learned not to share information on subjects my husband did not believe in.

Smiling at Larry's idiosyncrasy, I set off across the back yard to harvest red huckleberries. After squeezing (with considerable difficulty) through the aperture between the Kissing Boulders, I climbed the switchback footpath up the cliff which I had discovered in my childhood wanderings. Although sticking like a fly to the rocky side of the bluff had been much easier for a small child than it was for a woman three times her former size, the thought of red huckleberry jelly made the risk worth it. The huckleberries were fat and ripe that day–not as robust as blue huckleberries, but clearer, purer, tangier in taste. I soon filled my plastic buckets, filled myself with as many huckleberries as my stomach could hold, and started back down the bluff. I caused several small avalanches in my descent, but I managed not to fall. More important, to me, I kept hold of those buckets.

Back in the safety of my kitchen, I dumped a load of berries into the big colander in the sink, rinsed them, left them to drain, then removed my dusty shorts and tee shirt and tossed them into the washer on the back porch. I took a hot bath before I turned on the washer, then donned a flimsy muumuu that used to interest Larry when we were first married. Always hoping.

I had only enough red huckleberries for a few small jars of jelly, but that small batch held some kind of mystical significance for me: I believe I thought if Larry ate some of the jelly unawares and liked it, I could get him to believe a truth I knew and he denied. There were many lovely things I knew to be true and Larry believed were figments of my imagination. Perhaps converting to red huckleberries would be a first step to broadening his vision of Truth–and his vision of me.

When I had finished cooking the berries and sealing the jars, I washed and dried my mother's pressure cooker and set it on the counter by the back door. When she brought Bertie back after his beach adventure, she would want it--not that she would be doing any more canning this year. It was the principle of the thing. "Never a lender or a borrower be," she would quote Polonius, adding, "But if you borrow it, bring it back home soon to me." I set the jelly jars to cool on the kitchen window sill over the sink. Then I submerged my rubber spatula, wooden spoon, two small sauce pans, and all the other paraphernalia I had used to make the jelly into a sink full of suds. With my hands swirling suds around, I gazed at the jars on the sill: Some for my parents, some for my in-laws, some for my household, and some leftover for someone special, as yet undetermined. Rinsing and draining the dishpan, I sighed for a job well done and considered how strange it was that, though those jars of jelly were as beautiful to me as any work of art, I was determined that the jars of red huckleberry, blackberry, gooseberry, currant and blackcap jams I had put up that week would be my last curtsy to old-fashioned housewifery. When they had cooled, I would take the tray full of jars down to the fruit cellar under the house–my last household duty before Larry left on his trip and I began painting again in earnest.

Knowing it was going to be a really hot afternoon, I did not change out of my muumuu but kicked off my satin slippers and returned to the kitchen to fill a large tray with the canned jellies I had put up in the last week. Though morning had long passed, the kitchen still held a chill, and I was barefoot and braless. I could easily have put on a bra without removing my muumuu, but I preferred to leave Larry with a mental image of me in something flimsy. Maybe the memory of me standing in the kitchen in my almost-see-through dress might give birth to other images and, when he returned from his trip, he might sweep me into his arms, carry me to bed and make love to me with the hunger returning hunters are supposed to have. The linoleum floor felt wonderfully cool on the soles of my feet and I did a giddy little dance to celebrate my imminent freedom and the possible renewal of Larry's love.

I was still wearing the sheer muumuu when Nick showed up at the back door. And I was dancing. When I saw Nick's face framed in the window, my first thought was, "I am not wearing a bra and Larry will be back soon!" I could scarcely run back into the bedroom and put on a sweater. Nick was looking at me right through the window of the kitchen door. I threw one arm over my chest, supported my other elbow on it and, in that contrived position, tried to wave hello to Nick without setting my nipples bobbing at him. Then I opened the door.

"Excuse me for arriving unannounced," Nick grinned.

"I saw you earlier down by the river," I babbled. "Have you been here the whole time?"

"I went home to get something. See? I come bearing gifts."

I was grateful Larry had already left to shop for his trip. He would have been annoyed if his school friend, Nick, had passed the boundaries of our place without announcing himself first.

Nick handed me two fish frozen in aluminum wrap. Salmon, by the size and shape of them.

"Phonograph record?" I guessed. "Tie? Pair of slippers?"

"Water skis for your boy," Nicky laughed.

His eyes were merry when he glanced at my arms, which I had folded across my breasts in an attempt to cover them. I was certain Nick could read how long my sexual dry spell had been right through the thin muumuu.

"You want to put the fish on the counter?" I asked.

"I think they should be put in the freezer," Nicky suggested, stepping into the kitchen to present them to me.

To open the freezer door, I would have to lift my arms from my chest. Nick was holding his mouth funny to keep from laughing. That made me laugh and I snatched the fish from him, pressing them to my breast.

"Wow! That's not going to help," I exclaimed, jerking open the freezer compartment and shoving the fish inside. In one motion, I slammed the door closed and grabbed my coverall apron from the back of a kitchen chair.

"Are you going around giving fish to all your neighbors today, or are you hoping to bribe us into leasing land to you?" I joked, dropping the apron over my head and tying it firmly behind my back.

Nick blushed.

"That bribe thing you said," he admitted. "I *was* hoping to talk you and Larry into sealing the deal today. By the look of it, that plot down by the river is ready to be plowed under today to prepare it for planting winter vegetables."

"Look," I said, sitting at the kitchen table, tugging the top hem of my apron up towards my chin and motioning for him to sit across from me, "I'm ready to seal the deal on your renting the bottom land and on your doing the other stuff you proposed as well."

"I could grow some fine strawberries where that orchard stands;" he mused. "Bulldoze the trees, burn them and the vermin they house, plow all that luscious apple compost under and lease the land from you."

"Though it's pretty right now, the orchard should probably go, but Larry just says, "Too expensive.""

"With those trees out of the way, you might even have a view of the Columbia."

"If we stood on the roof," I laughed. "I hope we can convince Larry to cooperate about razing the orchard. I warn you, though, he's kind of possessive about those useless trees."

"I, on the other hand, am just a practical farmer who hates to see good land not bearing sound fruit–or vegetables, as the case may be."

"I'll try to convince him, really. I've always had mixed feelings about those warped old trees since my mother first warned me, 'Never, ever go anywhere near that orchard!'"

"Bet you did when you were a kid though."

"Only once, when she dragged me in under those creepy branches. She pointed out all the broken hunks of wood lying all over the place. 'You could trip on one of them and break your leg,' she said. 'There are hundreds of decaying trees in this orchard and all the brush and foliage would muffle your calls for help. You would lie here in rotting leaves up to your nose in spiders and ants–oh, and beetles!--crawling all over your skin, and no one would know you were here until your voice had dwindled to a froglike croak from screaming for help.' Then she dragged me back out of the orchard and I never went in there again–except one other time when I ran through as though pursued by the Hounds of Hell."

"Whew. For your peace of mind, I hope Larry does let me bulldoze the orchard."

"After he had proposed that you lease some of it, he began to worry, I think, that any transaction with only my signature on it would reflect badly on him somehow. Though my name is the only one on the deed, I'm still hoping to get his acquiescence. To keep peace in the family, you know?"

"Yeah, I'm a guy. I understand."

"So, until he comes around on his own," I said, getting up and moving towards the door.

"I should go cultivate my own cabbages," Nicky smiled, rising and taking his baseball cap out of his hip pocket. I glanced at his hips and sighed. Fortunately, at the time he was looking intently at one of my paintings which I kept hanging over the kitchen counter. "I get it," he chuckled.

The painting was a replica of the scene out the kitchen window right beside it.

"You do?" No one else had "gotten" it.

"But, wouldn't it have been easier just to have Larry put in a second window?"

I was pleased.

"That painting is my idea of true wit," I blushed. Larry had wanted me to take it down. He said, "It's aesthetically redundant. You've got the real landscape right there out the window. Why hang a fake version right beside it?"

Unlike Larry, Nick murmured, "Like looking at the same scene in a dream, or before your eyes are quite open in the morning."

"Larry says it's like looking out the window during a rain storm when you're half crocked."

"That's what makes it magical. The natural made supernatural."

"I painted it from memory while I was back east."

"That's some memory you've got," Nick whistled.

"I remember everything," I said, and we looked into one another's eyes for a quick moment. "My mother says she'd hate to have my memory for pain," I added, to divert attention from memories Nick perhaps shared with me. "Larry says he'd hate to have my memory for an injustice."

"Hmmm," Nick reflected, still looking at the picture. "Your paintings makes this farmer feel the way a good harvest feels. Complete."

"Wow," I said. I had no idea how to respond to such a generous comment. To cover my embarrassment, I changed the subject. "Larry's setting off on a fishing trip today," I said. "When he gets back, maybe he'll have a final answer for you."

We nodded at one another for a split second before he stepped out through the kitchen door.

"I'll call you when he gets back and we have had a chance to talk it over," I promised.

"Thanks."

"Oh, wait!" I said and ran back into the kitchen. I picked a round jar of red huckleberry jelly off the tray and took it out to Nick.

"Guess what flavor it is," I grinned.

Nick stared at the jar. "My mother and Donna used to put labels on everything they canned," he chided.

"I was about to do that when you interrupted me."

"A wild berry of some kind. Jar's still warm," he smiled.

"You don't remember my favorite?"

"Oh, red huckleberry!" he grinned. "One time you made me climb up this bluff here to pick them with you."

"And we got caught in a thunderstorm while we were up there," I remembered.

"How old were we, six?"

"About that. You saved me that day."

"You saved me. Showed me that shallow cave behind the huckleberry bushes where we could shelter from the storm."

"I was going to climb down the bluff in the driving rain. You saved me by telling me a story your grandmother taught you."

"Amaterasu and the storm god. About how the sun goddess is all mad at her brother, the storm god, and hides in a cave."

"The world gets as cold as we were that rainy day."

"But the people shine a mirror in the cave and Amaterasu is drawn out of hiding by her own reflection."

"By the time the story was over, the rain had passed and we safely climbed down the bluff."

"That path still there?" he laughed.

"How do you think I got to these red huckleberries?"

"You should have had Larry get them for you. You got some scratches on your ankles."

Someone still looks at my ankles?

"I never told anybody about that path but you, Nick."

He raised his eyebrows, but I did not answer whatever question was in them.

"I remember watching you pop the first huckleberry you found into your mouth," he said. "I was afraid you were going to fall off the bluff and die."

"Larry had the same reaction to red huckleberries," I laughed. "He still doesn't believe they exist."

"Please don't mention our red huckleberry orgy on the bluff then, or he may not let you call to tell me I can go ahead with my farming scheme."

"I won't, or, I mean, I will call you, or he will call you, if..."

"If he needs to do it himself. I know. I'm a guy, remember?"

"Not likely to forget that," I mumbled.

"What?"

"Like your hat," I smiled.

He smoothed the worn crown of his cap over his thick black hair, then walked backwards down the driveway towards his truck. Still grinning, he wheeled around and almost stepped into the open cellar stairway.

"Watch out, Nick!" I warned. "Those cellar steps are steep."

"You're not kidding," he laughed, side-stepping the hole. "You ought to keep that door shut."

"That's what Larry said when I asked him to open it for me last night. He interrogated me for a quarter hour about why I was going down cellar."

"Down cellar?" Nick laughed. "You say that too? I never knew why he used that expression."

"He spent summers with his grandparents back east, remember? He picked the expression up from them. And I picked it up from him."

"And you picked it up from him." Nick tilted his head and gave me an assessing look.

"I can't even lift the cellar door off its prop. He'll close it before he leaves on his fishing trip."

"Meantime, you ought to put some traffic cones around that gaping hole," Nick chuckled as he climbed into his truck.

"I don't get that many visitors."

"When I'm tilling your land, I'll wave at you every day so you don't feel lonely," he called out the truck window.

"I'm an artist," I laughed. "We don't get lonely, or, if we do, we paint a picture of it."

"Paint a picture of me sometime then, will you? Maybe I'm a little bit lonely." As he waved and drove away, I believe he added, "I'll pose for you." He did not know how often he posed for me in my head.

Just before his truck went out of sight beneath the branches arching over River Road, he stuck his head out the window and called back to me: "By the way, I saw the phantom lurking in the trees in that picture by the sink. I've seen them all."

He really gets my paintings!

Holding my apron and my thumping heart in place, I waved till Nick's truck disappeared. Then I went back inside to label my fruit jars and to pack a sack lunch for Larry to eat on the way to Central Oregon. But first, I leaned my belly against the sink and looked at my picture of home by the window, with its dark-eyed monster lurking in the pear tree.

❧

I Can't See My Feet

Before Larry returned from picking up the supplies that would make him the Complete Camper, I picked up my last tray full of jam and jelly jars. They would make a heavy load for me, but I liked seeing them all together like that, filling the large tray perfectly, except for the space where Nick's jam jar had been. I knew I should probably wait for Larry to carry them down cellar, but I wanted to complete every step of my canning alone, all at once. Mama and Larry had teased that I would get tired of canning after the first day--if I did not blow up the pressure cooker first. I grinned in triumph over my family's low opinion of my housewifery. Passing out the back door and through the porch, I kicked the door ajar with my foot and held it open with my hip while I negotiated the tray past the screen. Proud of myself for having almost filled the cellar shelves with canned produce in one summer, I walked down the slender sidewalk from the back door to the cellar carrying the tray high on my chest the way a drum majorette carries her baton.

I stood at the top of the stairs with that last tray of jam and jelly, not yet certain I could gather the courage to enter the root cellar by myself. Larry used the workbench down there to repair his lawn mower and occasionally to tinker with automobile parts, but no woman had used the earthen basement beneath Bertie's bedroom since my mother had kept it crammed full of home-grown canned goods during World War II. My arms were aching before I took even one step down cellar, but I bit my lip and reminded myself that only such a heroic act would impress Larry and my mother with my competence as a householder. I would have done better not to have been so stubborn.

The cellar door–broad and lying at a forty-five degree angle from the driveway up to Bertie's bedroom window–gaped wide at my feet. When Grampa had built the original cabin where the house now stood, the door had been constructed of heavy timber, and was later reinforced with metal to keep bears and raccoons out. The night before, it had taken all Larry's strength and a fat crowbar to open the cellar door so I could put the last of my canning in it today. He propped the door open against a tall pear tree stump next to the cellar door so it would be easier for him to push the door closed after I had stowed my last batch of jam. The house might rock on its foundations when the door crashed closed, but all my produce would be safe from possible marauders. The occasional bear still visited cabins on the lower Silky, and, though only rarely did they come into anyone's yard, our place was more remote than most. And who knew whether bears could smell berries vacuum-locked in Mason jars?

Or, worse yet, your little Injun buddies could steal our canned fruit.

Larry! They wouldn't do that. Not the same thing at all as picking up a few unwanted windfall apples.

Probably not, but it's a short walk from the orchard to the house, my dear.

As I am not fond of entering close, dark enclosures, I was still standing halfway down the stairs looking into the dark cellar when Larry came back from shopping for his trip. He hooked a sharp left into the parking space beside the cellar entrance, and a fine spray of gravel shrapnel peppered the backs of my arms and legs. Even before he stepped--too carefully--out of his truck, and before I saw the open beer can sticking out of a mound of ice in the open chest on the front seat, I knew he had been sampling some of the supplies he had just purchased.

"Not finished playing Little House on the Prairie yet, Canning Girl?" Larry teased.

I laughed, because I always found Larry's sarcasm funny, and because I was glad to see him. At his appearance, however, my apprehension about going down those stairs seemed to increase tenfold. Like the kid who scrapes her knee but does not cry until her mother appears, I felt my lower lip begin to quiver and tears to fill my eyes. That shows how much I hate enclosed spaces, but there was something else. Now that Larry had arrived, I no longer felt the urge to prove myself by braving the depths of the cellar. Besides, I was afraid I would fall on the way down there, and all my beautiful jars of jelly would break. Even if he had been half-crocked--and he was nowhere near drunk--Larry could more easily carry the tray down cellar than I could. That was probably really why I had hurried to finish my canning before he left. As much as I wanted to prove myself to him by actually facing that dark hole in the ground, I preferred that he take the canning down cellar and close the cellar door. It was a very heavy tray, after all. I should have taken the jars down those stairs one at a time. Standing in one place, I could hardly keep hold of the tray, and, when carrying it, I could not see the steps on the way down. The stairs carved into the earth had been replaced by concrete ones when my folks had the house raised and placed on a cement foundation, but many of the steps were crumbly along the edges. Even watching carefully, I had slipped more than once on them.

"I'm so glad you came back just now. Would you mind carrying this tray down cellar?" I called out to him. "It's so heavy, I'm afraid I'll drop it."

"When I come home, could you possibly wait one second before giving me my next household task?" Larry said as he blew by me up the walk.

"Sorry. I was just..."

"Do you mind if I get my bag first?" Larry said, grabbing the screen door handle. "And something to snack on during the drive."

"I packed a lunch for you. It's in a sack on the kitchen counter right by the back door."

"Thanks!" he called with a happy grin, as he jerked open the screen door.

"This tray is very heavy!" I complained.

"Then stop standing there with it and take it down cellar," he called, disappearing into the back porch.

"I can't see my feet!" I wailed, but he was already in the house by that time.

He took what seemed a very long time before coming to rescue me from the predicament I had gotten myself into. My arms were aching so that I thought I would drop the tray where I stood. I tried to step down to the next step but, feeling around with my foot, could not even find the tread. I was about to sit down on the step with the tray on my lap and set the jars one at a time on the step beside me when Larry emerged from the house, tossed his bag in the back end of his pick-up and his lunch sack in through the driver's side door. When he approached me, I reached out to him with the tray, my arms quivering. He put up his hands to stop me.

"You can do it, Kory. You took several trays down there already."

His voice identified him as the patient, amused, caring mentor. I, the unwilling, dubious disciple, responded.

"The tray is twice as full this time," I whined. "And you were with me then."

"To prove to you that you could do it without me, my little termite," he chuckled.

"I'm about to drop this one!"

"No, you aren't. Come on. I'll talk you through this. Left, right, left, right!"

I closed my eyes and stepped down to where I thought the next step was. It was not.

"I can't find my footing."

"Dip your foot a bit further," Larry urged. "You're almost there."

With him talking me through it, one agonizing step at a time, I managed to get within a few steps of the bottom before the spectacle of a full-grown woman holding a tray of clanking glasses and quivering with fright at the prospect of entering a harmless hole in the ground was too amusing for Larry to resist.

"There's more jelly in her legs than in her jars, boys," Larry laughed to his imaginary bar buddies.

I laughed nervously in response while the jars bounced and plinked against one another. "My arms are turning to jelly too, Larry. Help!" I gasped.

"Ladies and gentlemen," Larry announced at the top of the stairs, "The lady is in a real jam this time. "Good God, I believe she's turning to jelly right before our eyes." Then he sang dolefully, in his deep voice, *"J-E-L-L-OOOOH."*

My knees were shaking like the Scarecrow's on his way to Oz, and Larry was laughing so hard I could not help but laugh even harder.

"Stop laughing and help me. Take the tray!" By then, I was shaking all over while the jelly jars clanked a tune. My arms were breaking and I feared I would drop my beautiful jellies. I was about to turn and offer the tray to him one last time when Larry emitted a playful *Boo* behind me.

I suppose because I am goofy about close spaces, I did not at first perceive the cry as coming from Larry. Hearing the echo rising from the cellar, I flinched away from the dark recess. At the same moment, my arms gave out, the tray bounced off the tread, and tray, jars, and all my beautiful jellies and jams caromed into the cellar. Twisting to catch them on the fly, I lost my balance and skidded, one jagged concrete step at a time, to the cellar floor. As the floor and walls were dirt, fortunately, most of the jars did not break. I got some scrapes on my legs and arms and the crash made a terrific noise.

"Kor-eee! Are you being klutzy on purpose?" Larry scolded as he always did if I hurt myself.

"Sorry," I muttered, reaching around me to replace some of the jars on the tray.

"I am supposed to be on vacation, and instead I'm trying to teach my wife how to walk out of a cellar," he sighed.

"Fishing is not a vacation!" I reminded him, looking up at him from my supine position in the cellar dirt. "You said so this morning!"

"Damn, Kory, what a mess you've made."

"Don't worry, I'll clean it up." Pushing against the dirt floor with my palms to regain an upright position, I ground some glass shards into my hands.

"Don't be stupid. Take my hand," he said, reaching down the steps towards me, but just before he touched the tray, his fingertips stiffened.

"Is that unripe huckleberry jelly I see on that tray, Kory?"

"No."

"It says huckleberry right there on the label."

"It says Red Huckleberry," I corrected him. "Or, unripe huckleberries. Call them whatever you want. Just help me clean them up, please."

Larry just stood there looking down at me while I raised myself to my haunches and, on wobbly legs, started using a Mason lid to scrape up chunks of jam-shrouded glass and tossing them onto the tray.

"I passed Nick Nakamura on the way here," Larry mentioned, leaning casually against the open cellar door.

"He wanted to ask about that land down by the river again," I explained, wondering where the cool wind that was playing with the wispy hairs on the back of my neck had come from. I focused on scraping glass shards off the tray into a mouse hole against the dirt wall.

"And you greeted him in that dress?" Larry asked.

I was using the Mason lid to scrape the last of the glass shards into the mouse hole and did not look up at my husband. I was hoping the mouse was not at home.

"I covered up the dress with this apron. He couldn't have seen anything unless he has x-ray eyes." I began to set the jars that were unbroken back on the tray.

"He has got x-ray eyes," Larry smiled the way he did when recalling one of his teenage hijinks with Nicky Nakamura.

37

I carefully positioned the last jam jar on the tray and carried the tray to the shelves at the end of the workbench in the back of the cellar, shuddering as the wooden underside of Bertie's bedroom floor washed over me like a tidal wave. I could not help holding my breath. Turning towards Larry, I shivered, "I could drown in all this lightless air."

"What did you talk to Nick about?" he replied.

"Whether I wanted to lease some farm land to him."

"Whether *you* wanted to, Kory?" Larry asked. I had started up the steps, but his tone stopped me. He was incredulous. "Who drowns out the moles on *your* land? Who shoots the rabbits in the vegetable garden? Who pays the fucking property tax?"

"You do, Larry. I would help with expenses, but you don't want me to work."

"Work at what?" he asked. "Painting pictures?"

Here it was, one of the points of contention that had our marriage by the throat. Meanwhile I was becoming increasingly aware of the dark of the cellar pressing through the back of my thin dress and the dirt from the floor working its way up between my bare toes.

"I sold some paintings during my gallery days, back east."

"So, you paint pictures for other men and go around my house in a mangy old duster and an old lady apron."

Silence would have been a wiser answer, but with my back to a dark cellar I was edgy and could not help myself. I took off the apron and let it drop. "I wore this dress this morning because you once said it was your favorite and I wanted you to want to make love with me before you left on your trip."

Ignoring this painful domestic revelation of sexual hope and rejection, Larry squatted at the head of the stairs. I had the urge to shrink backwards into the cellar, but that was not a pleasant option either. With a disquieted man before me and a dark hole behind me, I was caught between fire and the grave.

"Why did you entertain Mr. Nakamura this morning?"

"I didn't. He brought us two salmon...."

"You promised him the farm, didn't you?" Larry lurched to his feet and took hold of the cellar door for support. I could see his hand was shaking.

"I thought you were interested in his leasing land from us?" I asked, confused.

"But you didn't check to see if I had changed my mind," he said, shaking his head in dismay.

"I told him I'd have to discuss it with you. He was perfectly happy to wait for an answer until your return."

"I'm always glad to see Nick perfectly happy," Larry said and began to try to pull the cellar door away from its supportive tree stump. It was so heavy, though, that he had to use two hands to jerk it into the upright position. Believing he was signaling me to hurry up the stairs so he could close the door behind me and be on his way, I quickly turned to pick up the empty tray, tucked it under my arm, and turned back towards the stairs. But, looking up at Larry, I paused. He was not a huge man, but standing at ground level when I was several steps below him in a deep pit, he blocked out half the sky and most of our large cherry tree. I hesitated.

"Jesus, Kory, don't look so stricken. I'm just a man holding a door for his wife."

Breaking my rule not to look in the eyes of men when they might be angry at me, I looked up into his face to try to parse his mood. His big cow eyes were glistening and it was no trick of the light. My heart went out to him. He had looked just that way when he had reported on the first forked-horn he shot. He had come to my folks' house especially to tell me he would never hunt deer again. Something in me–some incorrigible simplemindedness–rises to the surface in such situations, and I think I should be completely honest.

"You frighten me when you get upset, Larry," I whispered, feeling in my dress pocket for some weapon to wield against my fear. I found only lint, which I rolled into a tight ball with my fingertips.

"Upset about what?" he asked, at a loss.

"Me?"

"I'm not upset. Where do you get that?"

"You look upset."

"It must be the anticipation of unripe huckleberries puckering my mouth."

I had to laugh at the face he made. Larry could have made me laugh during an airplane crash. Maybe I found his sarcasm so hilarious because it seemed incongruous in such a solemn man.

"The ants on the cellar floor seem to like the jam," I joked, edging away from the insects which were swarming over a glob of jam close to my bare feet.

"I was only trying to explain a husband's gustatory preferences, Kory. What's so amusing about marital communication?"

"Just about everything, don't you think?" I giggled. Maybe it was my claustrophobic panic or that thumping my head took on the dirt floor that caused me to laugh, but the idea of fighting about huckleberries was getting more hilarious by the second.

"Did you also think it was funny to flirt with the local Casanova?" Larry teased.

"I was purposely not flirting with Nick," I blurted. Larry took the implications of that unfortunate revelation full in the chest.

"Purposely not flirting? You know, Kory, disloyalty can destroy a family forever."

"Okay, Larry, let me come up and explain," I said. My voice betrayed the dread I felt with all that darkness grabbing at me from the cellar.

"Come ahead," he said.

He reached one hand down to welcome me from the cellar, while with the other hand he still gripped the cellar door he had jerked from its support post.

"Come on," he beckoned. "I'd like to get to the lake before midnight."

I took a step upward.

"Just don't expect your lowly weatherman husband to hold the door open for you."

He let go of the door as he turned away, and it plummeted from its upright position, falling shut with a crash in my face.

Bad Things Happen to Girls Who...

I was on the way up as the door was on the way down, and, with the force of a pick-up truck crashing through a cement wall, it landed just inches from my head. The door sent a foreshadowing rush of hot August air into the cool cellar before it, and the wind of the plummeting door hit me with such force that I fell to my knees, certain that the doorjamb would splinter and I would be flattened on the dirt floor, crushed by the door itself. But, it was not the wind or the door that flattened me face down on the floor. It was the absence of light, the absolute dark of being shut into the earth. Later, when my eyes adjusted, I would be able to see light sifting in through cracks around the door frame and through the small ventilation grill in the concrete foundation of the house. But, in those first moments, I was blind as a mole in a hole, and the darkness strangled my lungs and heart. Still, I had breath enough to scream and scream, from the moment the door fell until the moment I thought I heard the scramble of tires on gravel. Or, I would have heard the sound, if I had not been screaming like a bagpipe in heat. When I went quiet in order to listen, I could no longer hear a car, but only my own screams echoing in my ears.

Then, silence. And the crushing darkness. The urge to scream some more was almost overwhelming, but I forced myself to listen for Larry's pick-up–for Larry.

"Larry?" I finally ventured, lifting my head and staring stupidly up at where I thought the door must be. Time passed.

"Oh!" I said. A laugh exploded out of me as a bulb bursts into light in a dark place. "It's a joke!" I exclaimed, pushing myself to my knees. In an ecstasy of relief that my husband was only playing one of his amusing tricks on me, I did not feel the glass shards pressing into my skin. Nobody could divert me with laughter the way Larry could. How he loved to put me in my place with a quip and a tweak on the cheek.

"Open Sesame!" I chortled. Sesame did not open.

If he was putting me in my place, why would he think my place was the cellar anyway? He had lived with my claustrophobia for years. Who would know better that it was the last place I would choose to be?

He must just be pulling my leg, I reassured myself. He always teased me about my phobias. This time he must have driven his truck down the lane and crept back to await my reaction. All I would have to do was to *have* a reaction and I would be as good as free. If there is anything as good as free.

"Knock-knock!" I cried.

Larry loved knock-knock jokes, but failed to answer right away, so I answered for him.

"Cellar dweller."

No answer but my own.

"Cellar dweller who?" I called.

Larry remained mum.   I completed my joke without assistance.

"If you can say cellar dweller ten times fast without tying up your tongue, I'll tell you who's there."

Larry did not try the tongue twister, so I did. "Cellar Dweller. Cellar Dweller. Sweller Deller." Two repetitions were my limit. I laughed and no one laughed with me. I knelt and knelt alone, soaking in the silent rebuff. I felt the dirt wall behind me gathering itself to burst across the small room and crush me. *Damn cellar can't take a joke*, I cringed.

"Larry? Come on, the joke wasn't that bad. I hear crickets chirping." I heard no crickets, though I feared I would later, if the temperature dropped to fifty degrees–or whatever the cutoff point for the cricket chorus was–and if the unthinkable happened and I was still in the cellar at the time. I squeezed myself into a quivering ball on the dirt floor at the mere thought.

Within seconds, I lifted my head. I thought I heard the crunch of pick-up tires on the gravel driveway. Then a car door slamming.

"Larry, open this door!"

Why play such a mean trick anyway? *To evoke my usual good-sport response, of course.* Larry had married me for my good cheer. *Certainly not for sex.* He liked my readiness to make a joke or to laugh when he uttered the mildest witticism.

"Ally, ally oxen free!"

That would make him chuckle. If he heard it. Maybe he had put his truck in neutral and coasted to the bottom of the drive. *Louder, Kory.*

"I'm too scared to think of any more bad jokes, Larry!"

Not that I was afraid of him, really. What I was afraid of was small dark rooms.

"No kidding, Larry, are you still out there?"

Only the dark cellar answered, sending a puff of its cold breath onto the back of my neck. If I had not depended on the certainty of Larry's opening the door before long, I would have sunk into a coma from fear of that modest hole in the ground. Though, I never coordinated his fishing ensemble to his standards, I loved and trusted Larry more than almost anything. The reason was that I knew him. He was dependability personified. Besides, his body made our bed smell good. True, I loved our child with a purer love, but I never made that comparison aloud.

"Hello?"

He must know I could not budge that heavy door, and he would not have driven off without opening it for me. He would come back sooner or later to check the door for damage. That would be his way of apologizing for scaring me witless. That might take a few minutes, though, and I wanted out of the cellar now. With hands over eyes, I closed out the darkness and tried to imagine the light. Imagination failing, I began to panic in earnest.

"Larry, for goodness sake," I squealed, "This is not a good joke. Open the door. Larry, help me. We both know I can't open this door."

I listened but all I heard was the hot August wind scraping the apple trees' scaly limbs against one another.

The sound reminded me that neglected living things–orchards, people–decay and die. The apple trees had been doing it for decades. I figured it would not take nine days for one woman locked in a cellar to do it.

Sounds of gravel spraying and tires screeching as some vehicle turned where the bottom of the driveway met the dirt end of River Road.

"Larry?" *Or, just someone who failed to read the Dead End sign at the junction to River Road?*

The sounds of tires on our rutted road diminished into dust.

"Larry!"

If a woman calls her husband's name when he's not there to hear it, is he anything but a word dissolving in air?

"All right, Larry. You are in for it now. I will take you down like a rootless tree in a windstorm."

Such comical imprecations I had thrown at him when he was trying out his wrestling holds on me in college. I would puff myself up, hurl myself at him, and he would flip me onto the grass with a flick of his wrist. I would laugh like a loon, struggle to my feet and start all over again. The result was always the same. *Is that the game today, Larry?*

Despite my daring words, I had not puffed myself up this time. I had not even stood myself up. Why had I not moved since collapsing under the initial descent of the door? *I'm waiting.* I knelt there, one knee on the concrete margin below the stairs, the other on the earthen floor of the cellar, waiting.

For what?

There was no question of Larry leaving me shut in the cellar, of course.

He'll come back.

He could be a testy fellow, but he was a gentleman, after all. If I was carrying two bags of groceries or our child or a heavy chair, Larry would always open the door for me and shut it behind me. Though he was not a slave to tradition and would not

45

open a door for me if I could do it perfectly well by myself, Larry was the sort of person who considered it his manly duty to do those little things for women and other weaker beings that they could not do for themselves.

Sentimental tears burned my eyes at the thought of my handsome husband taking a long step to get ahead of me and open a door for me, at the Junior Prom, the Senior Prom, the grocery store, the hospital where I was about to give birth to our son. *How many doors has he opened for me?* I could just see him stepping up to the cellar as the prince stepped up to Snow White's casket, and stooping to wrench the whole cellar door from its frame in his eagerness to free me. *Thank you, Prince.* There was no question of his not opening the door. I remained where he had left me, listening for the return of his pick-up truck whose rough purr I knew as I knew the sound of his heartbeat.

When the door did not open in five seconds, ten dark seconds, half a minute of loathing the absence of light, five minutes of terror, I recommenced my screaming. But, my throat was soon so sore that I realized I had strained my vocal cords--an occurrence that would repeat cyclically throughout my stay in the cellar. I decided to save my voice for a time when I knew for sure someone was near enough to hear it. Besides, I did not want to repel my rescuer with what he might take to be hysterical female screeching. Instead of shouting, I wrapped my arms around my chest and squatted on the mud floor like a crumpled piece of origami art depicting a suppliant pleading for deliverance. Tears and self-pity came blossoming out of my bones. I folded my shoulders down to my knees and hacked like a pet dog who has had its vocal cords cut because the neighbors complained of his barking. I was probably expressing the same thing the voiceless dog says: *Hello! Hello! Is anybody outside this door? Let me out. I'm meant to run free. Open it, please, and let me out. Hello!*

Finally, I chanced a stingy squint and peered to the right and left. The cellar was as dark and empty as Jesus' tomb after the Ascension, but I felt the shaming presence of a party of family and friends skulking in the impenetrable corners of my mind--or of the room, I could not always tell them apart in the cellar. I was remembering, how, in the good days when we were first married, Larry would never criticize or tease me when we were alone. He saved the best of his wit until a large cast of extras was on the set with us. One of his favorite scripts was on the theme of my fear of closets.

"Kory applies her make-up at the kitchen table and showers with the window wide open for all the world to see. (True.) She hates closets so much she hangs her coats and our child's parka on a coat tree, and hangs the rest of her clothes on hooks outside our bedroom closet. (All true.) Unlike a normal husband, I have to hang up my own apparel--if I want to keep it in a closet. So far, this is only a charming quirk of my wife's. But, if I *ever* catch her sleeping outdoors in a tree like an orangutan, I'm going to have to keep her locked up in a cage and just toss her a banana once in a while."

A laugh gurgled out of my throat and a bubble of spittle made a miniature puddle in the mud under my chin. Even from my lowly perspective, I had to admit Larry did a pretty great imitation of a sissy girl orangutan. Laughing caused me to raise my face out of the dirt, and, taking advantage of the momentum, I pushed my palms against my thighs, forcing myself to a kneeling position.

Where are you, Larry? Where is my hero?

Out looking for a banana to throw into your cage, Kory.

I blushed at the picture of myself which the memory of Larry held up to me in the dark. My anger stung like iodine on a bad scrape. I slapped my palm on the hard mud floor and tried to shout my anger. All that came out was a squeaky little girl voice.

No fair, no fair, no fair!

47

My palm stung as if with a thousand stab wounds.
Don't bang on the floor, Kory.

I tried to brush off the glass shards that had scattered when I dropped the tray, but I was only hurting myself. Those wounds would have to wait. My self-esteem was squirming from multiple contusions.

Bang on the door, Kory. Not on the floor.

Why had I not leapt to my feet the moment the door slammed shut, shouting and crying; pushing and banging at it in an attempt to get out? If someone else's wellbeing is at risk, I act immediately. Once, when I saw a child about to run in front of a car, I whisked her into my arms and carried her to safety. A dog chased and cornered a squirrel and I stood guard over the smaller animal until the snarling mongrel tired and sniffed up more available game. I have done such things. I am the kid who stood between the school bullies and the class cripple or brain or whoever else was the scapegoat du jour and gibbered at the little tyrants until they stopped attacking or the school bell rang. But, if I was in trouble, it always took me an eternity to turn around and help myself.

Now, as an unwitting participant in a mystifying event, what was I doing? I was kneeling beneath the implacable awning of a cellar door, and waiting for my husband to come rescue me was what I was doing. The irony of the picture I presented hit me suddenly: I was the unintentional victim waiting for the perpetrator to mutate into her rescuer. I began shaking like the cherry tree leaves which were quivering in the hot August wind beyond that closed door.

By now, a normal woman would have been banging on that cellar door for ten minutes straight.

"But I know I can't open it! I've tried," I answered myself.

Who can open it then, Kory? What are you waiting for?

"I evaluate life in pictures," I reasoned, prim in my ladylike kneeling position, "in case I should want to paint the scene before me. I'm afraid to move lest I jog my husband and myself out of the time frame of our last encounter. As long as I remain in the same pose I was in when Larry left, I can envision him coming back to complete the picture by opening the door again."

Action, not aesthetic claptrap is what's needed right now. Try banging on the door.

"I'm afraid to find out Larry actually shut the door tight and that I really can't push it open!"

I sat and thought about that revelation for a moment.

You won't know until you try, Kory. At least open your eyes.

"I hate to look at the dark."

You can't fix what you can't see.

Before I even fully lifted my lids, my eyes had begun adjusting to the darkness, and I could sense that a small amount of light was coming into the room. Maybe the door had already been opened. My eyelids lifted slower than Queen Victoria's hem. I was half hoping I would see Larry standing there, the door flung wide to free me. But I saw only a thin gruel of grey light spilling in through the vent on the north side of the foundation. Confronting the dim reality of my situation roused me from my lethargy.

"Larry!" I screeched, leaping to my feet and climbing the cement steps. My good screeching voice had come back momentarily, and I shouted and banged on the underside of the door with the heels of my hands, though I was pounding some remaining glass shards into them. "You come back here and let me out. Don't you dare leave me down here, Larry! Oh, my God, Larry!"

When pounding had no effect, I tried to push on the cellar door with a long, steady pressure. The door slanted over the steps so acutely, though, that there was really no good place for even a strong person to stand in order to push upward with effective leverage and open the door. If I stood on the bottom step, I could not reach the door. If I stood on the next step, I could not straighten my arms fully to press hard on the door. I tried my best though. I pounded, I pushed with desperation as if the darkness at my back were an amorphous monster pressing me, squeezing me, suffocating me with its musty paws. I slapped at the door with all the resentment in me, as if it were a bully who had belittled a smaller child in the school yard. The door did not budge.

I can't wait any longer, Larry! Hurry.

My knees gave way and I leaned against the concrete wall of the stairwell. I could feel the grain of the planks the workmen had used to mold the cement pressing patterns into my skin. Sobs collecting inside my forehead were pressing me to cry out loud. But I did not want to cry as I had the first time I had been shut in a dark place. That confinement–brief in the history of time but endless in the history of a little girl–had resulted in an extreme dislike for having doors slammed in my face. By the time I had been found, I was sleeping, exhausted from crying for hours, and I had not heard my potential rescuer.

Don't wear yourself out, Kory. You have to stay awake, in case someone comes by.

"For when Larry comes back. Now I remember, he turned away as the door was shutting. Maybe he doesn't even know I'm still in here!"

Yeah, because he wouldn't have heard the door slam with a clap like thunder.

"He had been drinking a little."

Exactly.

"What?"

Open your eyes. You'll figure it out.

"They are open, and I don't like what I see!"

The walls had come closer while I had my eyes closed, and the mud parameters of that small cellar had already been about as close as they could get. Now they continued their imperceptible march towards me. Looking around at my prison cell, I thought, *I am a four-star claustrophobe and I am trapped in a dark, cold hole underground.* If not for the wan light and trace of air

50

allowed in by the wire-mesh window in the northern wall of the house's concrete foundation, I thought, I would have slit my wrists with glass shards one minute in. As my eyes adjusted better to the vague light coming through the aperture, I felt pain in my knees and my palms where I had fallen on the broken jam jars. I was afraid to touch myself to see if I was bleeding, but my palms hurt where they had met the earth and I needed to assess my wounds. I felt as if every touch of my bare soles to the dirt floor signaled the walls to squeeze closer together, but I hobbled towards that shoe box-sized vent to examine my wounds in its feeble light.

Pressing my body against the dirt wall, I strained upwards towards the tiny window with its metal grill. Looking at the outdoors for the first time since the door had closed on me (it had probably been minutes, but it seemed hours), I could picture Larry driving towards his favorite fishing site in Central Oregon.

How far have you driven by now, Larry?

I could not help but listen for an answer. I tilted my ear upwards towards the metal mesh. Silence as absolute as the absence of an approaching savior.

Adjusting my position, I pressed my cheek against the wall, then jumped away from the window.

Things are moving in the dirt wall.

Who knew how many beetles, earthworms, grubs and slugs I was cohabiting with? I felt something move under my bare foot and leapt around like a novice fire walker.

Bad things happen to girls who run around barefoot like trailer-park people.

"You were right about some things, Mama."

Jumping around to avoid unseen crawly things made me aware that my physical hurts were considerable. With difficulty, I climbed up on the workbench. *Fewer bugs here, maybe.* Moving as close to the tiny cellar's glassless window as possible, I examined my wounds. My palms and fingertips had blood smeared on them. My right knee felt prickly and I knew the shards must have pierced the skin. The glass remaining in the wounds was commingled with dirt. I had picked up all the visible shards from the floor before I had fallen to my knees, so any glass in my knees or hands would have been too small for me to pick out in such dim light. I looked around me as if I could have espied some source of water to wash the wounds, but there are no faucets in dirt cellars.

What if he doesn't remember until he is all the way over the Cascades? The possibility that I could be confined in a small, dark space for hours came crashing down hard on me. I could feel the dirt walls falling in on me and covering me with tons of earth. No angleworm of an escape plan could have wriggled its way through all the dirt invading my mind. I was being buried in a process that had begun in the house overhead long, long ago. That feeling returned repeatedly during my stay in the cellar, increasing to an unendurable level until I purged it with door-banging or shouting or some other action that would have been excessive in any other context. Each time I had screamed myself silly, I would reassure myself that Larry would turn his pick-up around when he remembered. Then, like a flu-stricken invalid, I would feel well enough for a while to do what I could to survive until the next convulsion of panic.

But Larry would come rescue me. Surely, the bond between a man and a woman can stretch over a measly mountain range? *Besides, it is not in Larry's character to leave any loose ends lying around–such as a wife locked away somewhere.*

In the dim light, I could just discern a neat stack of newspapers on the southern end of the workbench. Larry had been using them to catch the oil under the lawnmower motor while he cleaned and repaired it on the workbench. There was not one page left awry in that stack. A man like Larry, who would probably have come all the way back across mountains just to straighten a stack of newspapers, would not continue with his fishing trip knowing he had not left his house in order.

"Keep your guns on the rack, your tools in a dry place and your wife barefoot in the kitchen."

Or the cellar? No, Larry! Maybe in your anger, you overlooked the fact that I cannot open the cellar door. That has to be what happened.

If I knew him, he would be mulling over what I had said while he drove, pounding the steering wheel with annoyance as he reviewed our last conversation. From past experience, I knew he would probably run the entire transcript of our disagreements over the years, from the time we first argued about the outfit I wore on a date when we were sixteen to the last words we spoke to one another.

Eventually, he would come to the transcript's end and, as he drove the heel of his hand into the steering wheel, he would remember how the cellar door had felt as he slammed his palm against it, thus shutting me into the root cellar.

Oh, hurry up with your interminable brooding, Larry!

When that happened, he would know he had accidentally imprisoned me for the extent of his hunting trip and he would turn the pickup around and come back to free me.

I'm waiting.

Shutting my eyes tight against the dark again, I played and replayed the little movie of my hero driving and driving, then realizing what he had done, and turning around to come save me.

How long are you going to wait for him to realize what happened, Kory? Until you starve to death, or die of the cold?

"It's August, and the cellar is stacked floor to ceiling with canned fruit."

August in Oregon can get cold at night, and how are you going to open the sealed food containers? Bring your fancy new electric jar opener down cellar with you, did you?

"Shut up, shut the heck up!"

53

I'm only asking.

I was not going to sit around arguing with myself about my husband's memory. He would be back soon enough to make all things clear. I decided to think about something else. There were plenty of pressing concerns to attend to when stranded in a room with mud walls. For one thing, I had all that blood to sop up somehow. As objectively as a nurse in a trauma ward, I decided not to blot the blood, but, lacking clean water, to let the blood wash the wounds. I could not crawl the length of the workbench to fetch the newspapers, because of the cuts on my knees. I crawled down from the bench, using the under-shelf like a step ladder. Then I scurried across the dirt floor, to prevent any tiny creatures from hitching a ride on my bare feet. With agility that amazed me, I climbed up close to the stack of newspapers. *Lady orangutan.* I laid a few sheets of the newspaper on the edge of the workbench beside me, and lifted myself onto the paper. I figured that sitting on sterile newspaper ink was the best way for someone to bleed glass out of her body without getting infected.

Proving I was starring in a bad melodrama, the phone in the kitchen upstairs rang. And rang.

"Hey, Larry, could you get that? I'm down cellar!" I choked on my own laughter.

The phone rang again.

"Hang up and come see if I'm all right!" I commanded. Then I felt silly. He would come check on me. He was a decent man. The thought of how sad he would be when he saw my wounds brought tears to my eyes. Like when he shot the forked-horn.

The phone stopped ringing after only four rings.

"Hasty, aren't we?" I shouted in the direction of the kitchen upstairs. "You didn't let it ring very long. If that was you, Larry, you better have hung up to come check on me."

I waited, imagining he was doing that. He was laughing about his ridiculous oversight.

I placed two small squares of paper on my knees

to absorb the blood, and splayed my hands out beside my hips on the newspaper which was serving as my seat cushion. Droplets of blood dried on the papers atop my knees and beneath my palms while I sat on the cellar work bench.

Still waiting.

No way was Larry going to leave something belonging to him exposed to the elements. He was too well-organized to let that happen.

What about the item he kicked into the grass that time? He forgot that soon enough.

"That was an inanimate object!"

They say that's how it starts.

One time, Larry had gotten so mad at our badly functioning well pump that he drop-kicked the heavy plumber's wrench he had been using to fix it. The wrench sailed only a couple feet into tall grass but later when he went looking for it he had no idea where it could be. He stormed around the house accusing me or Bertie—who could not, at that point, have lifted the thing—of misplacing it. Finally, I saw the blood soaking through Larry's tennis shoe. I put two and two together and found the wrench in the wreath of tall grass surrounding the pump house.

"Where'd you have it hidden?" he demanded when I handed it to him. He prodded me in the ribs with the thing. "Eh?"

"It was in the grass by the pump shed," I said.

"What the fuck was it doing there?"

"I think you must have kicked it there, Larry," I suggested.

"That's like saying I put a football in my tool chest," he snorted, wagging his head. Then he shook out his newspaper, folded it down the middle and resumed reading the day's news. I was certain he simply did not remember his toe striking that wrench and never would.

What if– in his anger--he blanked out the noise of the door slamming shut?

If so, would he ever remember he shut the cellar

door?

His memory of his own tantrums is not all that dependable, Kory.

"How long have I been down here?" I wondered aloud.

Too long for a man not to remember he left his wife in a hole in the ground.

The single benefit of being trapped in the dark was that I gradually became aware of new and subtle changes in light and shade in the cellar as the sun moved freely across the sky outside. Spending my days inside the house, I realized, I had adapted my work to the movement of the sun. I washed dishes when the sun was painting the trees and lawn on the kitchen side of the house. I sat at the sewing machine when the sun warmed its wooden work top. I made the beds as the sun passed the bedroom windows. A speedy replay of my day indoors would show me running from room to room to stay as close to the brightest light available at every minute.

Time is passing in my house and I'm not there to see it happen.

I preferred painting open vistas more than anything, and being shut in a small dark room was the worst punishment ever.

Punishment for what?

"For nothing!" I cried aloud. "Larry has only forgotten that his weakling wife is incapable of lifting that door by herself."

Oh, please! He can't have forgotten. Remember the shotgun?

A few months ago, I had been so desperate to find a safer place to keep his gun that I had tried unsuccessfully to open the cellar door in order to hide the gun from our son down there. I had actually got on my knees and begged Larry to put it in the cellar.

Larry can't have forgotten that mini melodrama.

"You can't even lift that door, he had laughed," and he was right.

"Then Bertie won't be able to lift it either," I said. "You have to open the cellar door and put your gun down there, please!"

"It would rust," Larry said.

He never did lock it up.

He *must* know I could never get the cellar door open. How could he have left me trapped like this? If I was depending on my husband to get me out of the pickle I was in, I might have to wait until he had an ice chest full of fish, or his nine-day trip was over.

I sat there with my legs dangling off the workbench and cried for the loss of the pretty picture in my head of the beau holding the gate for his damsel. That is one motif I would never depict on canvas again. I wracked my brain trying to recall a proper prototype for what I had to do. How does the damsel escape from her prison tower, or the witch's oven or her own casket without the handsome swain arriving to save her?

After considering that poser for a while, I leapt off my perch and squared away at the closed door.

"Considering Larry's possible motives will have to wait," I said, "Right now, I have to find a way out of here."

❧

Painting Murals on the Moon

Larry knew diddly squat about painting, but, between the two of us, he was certainly the expert on feats of strength. He was not a burly man, but had lifted weights until parts of him certainly approached burly. For laughs, I had tried to lift one of his weights once. No luck. Larry stopped his exercise routine to instruct me. He was always telling me my self-confidence needed honing, which had the opposite effect of making me feel increasingly unconfident about myself.

Bend your knees, Kory. Use those hefty thighs.

I could bend my knees till I was bowlegged and still couldn't lift one of your weights, Larry.

If your confidence were as hefty as your thighs--

They are not hefty. Are they? Even if they were, I'd have as much luck trying to lift the house.

Everything we do well is one part thigh and ninety-nine parts confidence, Kory.

By the time I had reviewed Larry's exercise routine, my eyes were accustomed enough to the dark that light framing the cellar door seemed like a neon sign outlining my target for me.

"I have lifted a husky preschooler singlehanded," I boasted to the door.

The door silently reminded me that it was heavier than my son Bertie, and that it was reinforced with iron.

Women have lifted cars off their children to save them. I can lift a door off a forty-five degree door frame to save myself.

I jumped off the bench again and tiptoed across the cellar to the cement steps. In my first panic after the door slammed on me, I had just flailed at the door. This time, using what Larry had taught me about strength, I would approach the problem more effectively. Even without Larry, I could figure out that I could not lift this obstacle from the tip top of the stairs, because, as I climbed the steps, I had to hunch over farther and farther due to the degree of incline of the door.   Hunched over in a stairwell, one does not have much leverage.

Bend your legs and use your thighs.

"I will have to bend more than my legs, Larry. I will have to bend my whole body into a flesh pretzel."

I sat on the third step and scooted on my bottom as far up the stairwell as I could. An image came into my head, of the lid of my mother's mangle pressing down on the Little Bo Peeps which decorated my favorite dress as a girl. I bowed my head low, bent my knees, hunched my shoulders up against the door and then, unbending my knees and using my thighs, pressed upwards against the door with as much strength as I could muster.

"I'm a pioneer woman!" I grunted, pushing again. The door did not give an inch. I scooted over closer to the latch and tried again. And again. Scuttling sideways like an oversized hermit crab, I moved all over the underside of the door and, time after time, pushed with my shoulders, then with my arms. I butted the door with my head until I ascertained that my head would split before the door did. I lay upside down with my back breaking over the ragged edge of the concrete step and pushed with my feet. In every position and with every part of my body possible, I pushed with long, steady pushes, short powerful lunges, and, finally--screaming imprecations--with pointless, thrashing punches. Then I cried aloud, as if the sound of sobs could open an iron-shod door. I swore at Larry and pounded at the door. I cried some more and stormed, and swore for what seemed an hour, but all I got out of it was a sore throat, bloodier hands, and a piercing headache from door butting. I fell onto the hard-packed dirt floor before the implacably shut door, with stinging tears flooding my sinuses. *This is a lesson Larry is teaching me. That's what this is.*

What's the lesson, Larry? I wept, but the answer was not revealed.

"No more tears," I finally declared. "There's a water shortage down here as it is."

Larry is not coming soon. Not before dinner time, in any case. Time to think up something I have a chance of doing for myself for a change.

But, what?

I could use a crowbar about now– even a rusty one. You would think a man would keep his tools where he used them, on his workbench. But, no. Larry kept them in a cabinet on the enclosed back porch to prevent them from rusting in the dank cellar.

What did Larry do for light down here anyway? I remembered him buying an extension cord as long as our garden hose and dragging the work-light he used when he worked on parts of his car down here–sanitizing his spark plugs or something. At the moment, however, the cord and light were coiled and hanging on the hook he screwed into the inside porch wall. So, my only illumination was the ventilation grill with its insipid northern light.

To prevent alerting the cellar vermin, I tippy-toed the few feet to the north wall and looked closely at the grid of wires. The wan glow from that tiny window would not have illuminated the hammering of a nail if it had a head the size of a platter. But was the vent big enough for me to squeeze through– if I could somehow remove the metal grill from the opening? I held my hands to my shoulders and then–keeping them the same width apart–held them up to the window. Maybe, if I hunched my shoulders together. Good thing I was not what you would call busty--not what Larry would call busty anyway. I performed the same careful measurement of my hips vis-à-vis the window. They were an inch or two narrower than my shoulders, but a good deal deeper. I might just be able to wriggle through that opening in the concrete foundation. Or, I might get caught halfway through and starve to death before Larry returned. To get out of that dank hole in the ground, however, I would certainly try, if I could somehow loosen the grill.

I climbed up on the workbench and knelt under the window. Ow. The glass cuts on my knees made that uncomfortable. I scooted along the workbench to Larry's pile of newspapers and placed some of them under the window as a kneeling pad. I only had to kneel for a few minutes to ascertain that the metal wires forming the grill were about a hundred times thicker than chicken wire and imbedded deep in the concrete foundation on the top, bottom and sides of the window hole. Hooking my fingers through the mesh–which featured about 3/4 inch openings–I tugged, wrenched, and jerked at the wire to pull it free from the concrete. I could as easily have grabbed a hunk of the foundation and ripped out a slab to fashion an escape hatch. I fell back on the workbench and wondered if experiences like this were what had motivated men of God to imagine the existence of Hell.

This was not hell, though. It was real life on earth and it was bearing down on me. I could feel my shoulders being crushed inwards as if the cellar had turned into a huge man who was squeezing me with arms like fir trunks. The weight of the cellar was pressing down on my back, my shoulders and the back of my neck, bowing me down till my forehead banged against the work bench. *I can't think about that. Can't think about being in and having to get out. Can't think about it.*

Still, the reality that I was stuck in a closed, dark place kept taking my breath away. The vent might as well have been filled with bricks for all the access it gave me to the open air. I had spent all my energy on the impossible task of pulling metal out of concrete, and the grumbling in my stomach made me realize I would not have the energy to do anything else to save myself until I had refueled.

You see, red huckleberries are not food, Larry chortled in my head.

Not much of a substitute for a Western omelet, I told myself. *And lunchtime was spent trying to escape*

*from the cellar. Better figure out how to "Open-sesame"
a sealed can or bottle of food.*

I sat with my arms wrapped around my bowed
head to hold off the dark while I plotted my next course
of action. For the present, I had done all I could to get
out. Now to forage in a root cellar for enough food to
last till my next escape attempt. Or, until someone came
to rescue me. *Dream on, Rapunzel.*

I turned my head towards the shelves full of
containers on the south wall. There was plenty to eat
within my reach on those shelves, which were filled with
the yield of my fall canning project. But what magical
formula could I devise to open one of those canning jars?
Though the jars gleamed only dully in the dim light of the
vent, the sight of them made my mouth water and my
empty stomach clench with pain. I had been so proud to
seal those rows of jars too tight for bacteria to invade
them or thieving varmints to steal from them. How I
would have laughed is anyone had told me the first
thieving varmint to steal the fruits of my labor would be
me.

Thank goodness for my ravaging hunger, as it
saved me from going crazy with dread that first afternoon
and evening.   I was getting so hungry that, even the
spilled jam lying in the dirt was looking good. By the
time I began to think of food, however, I noticed a
festival of movement was occurring on the jam. Of
course, if I were to be entombed long enough, I might
need the protein afforded by the bugs the jam would
attract. I laughed aloud at the idea I would ever eat a
bug, but stopped when I heard something skittering for
cover at the sound of my laughter. I had bare feet, so
even if I had felt desperate enough to walk across the dirt
floor again to get at the spilled jam, I would not have
chanced running into whatever creature I had just heard.
Meanwhile, every time I looked at my canned food
larder, the impulse to grab one of the jars and whack its
top off on the edge of the workbench all but overcame
me. If I did that, however, I was sure to die of incidental

glass shards I would ingest along with the food I had so lovingly prepared.

I would have to do something about my grumbling belly sometime soon though. All the jars of food contained–in addition to scads of nutrients–plenty of liquid, which, if I were to spend much time as a shut-in, I would surely need to imbibe in lieu of water. But, how to get at the edibles encased in sealed canning jars? The pears and cherries so carefully picked from the trees in our backyard were sealed with rubber rings, and atop those, flat lids, and finally--holding rubber and metal firmly in place--screw-on ring tops. How was I to open the jars without seasoning my supper with ground glass?

"If I had been jailed for my failings, I would at least be fed ill-prepared meals on a tin plate," I observed to the mud walls. At the sound of my voice, something skittered again, in the vicinity of my fruit shelves. Conjectures about what could be slalom racing amid my canning jars curbed my appetite for a while. The canned food still called to me, but I neither wanted to move through the suffocating darkness nor walk barefoot across the creepy vermin-filled earthen floor only to find some nondescript wriggler slathering and sharpening its claws on my pantry shelves. The growing pain in my belly however, eventually trumped my fear of tight spaces and underground creatures.

The one fact that would have been obvious to anyone who required her husband, or, in his absence, her own personal electric jar opener to open any sealed container, was that I was not going to be able to walk up to one of the jars on the shelf, wrap my fingers around the lid and open it. The second fact: unless you are a daughter of Hercules, you need some sort of tool to open a sealed container. Third: even I, with what Larry called my quixotic Ethos, knew I did not have such a tool in my muumuu pocket. Four: to find a tool in a dark, unknown place, you need a unique method to appraise the space and its possible contents.

63

Given that the cellar was creepy and no doubt teeming with hidden critters, I did not want to spend more time off my elevated workbench than necessary. Therefore, ignoring my roaring belly, I sat cross-legged high up on the work bench and mapped out a mental grid of the scene as if I were about to paint a small dark room with a jar-opening device hidden in it somewhere.

I was no engineer, but I had been taught by my mentor in the Art Department, Professor Groh, to analyze a scene without missing a fraction of an inch. She said, if an artist looked at any setting, he or she could feel the gravity of a hidden object weighing down one part of the scene. Dr. Groh could have been a detective, I always thought. She was like a water witch or dowser of lost or hidden items. To demonstrate her dowsing ability, she could look at a room and deduce in which drawer or cabinet or vase one of her students had concealed a key. I figured if I could deduce by the Groh method the most likely hiding places for potential tools to open my fruit jars, I could minimize actually touching the dirty places where vermin likely awaited me, while making certain not to overlook any potential hiding spots for jar-opening tools.

Eyes closed, I mentally surveyed the gloomy dirt floor and walls of my realm. With my artist's eye, I scanned and analyzed every segment on the grid and highlighted the segments that seemed to say *Lookee here, Lady!* I could only hope that the laws of good composition applied to power spots in a room as well as those in a painting. Now it seems a bit balmy, but at the time I was forced to work with the tools at my disposal. And, I was not a bad dowser of lost items myself. Witness my locating Larry's wrench, and many other misplaced items of friends and family over the years. With renewed self-confidence, I began my quest. Knowing I was probably only putting off the inevitable chore of crawling around on the dirt floor looking for potential tools, I scrunched my eyelids tight and tried to paint my way, mentally, out of the cellar. Maybe even the eccentric Professor Groh would have laughed.

The first place I searched was the bench on which I sat, not only because, as a work surface it was the most likely place to find any sort of tool, but also because I could search it while elevated from the earthen floor. Above ground, in a civilized setting, I could have held a tiny mouse in the palm of my hand, but below ground, I could only think of rodents as part of the writhing infested darkness in which I was trapped. I experienced the very cellar atmosphere as heavy claws rasping at the skin of my body. But, no matter how hard I tried to imagine that the tool I needed was within arm's reach atop my relatively safe workbench, my method broke down, and within minutes I was just searching anywhere that caught my eye. Moreover, my tool-locating mission had focused more of my attention on my hunger than on the cringing nerve endings in my skin, and I was hungrier than ever. I hated to think that what Larry always said about an education in the arts was true.

We need graduates who are preparing to build highways, levees and bridges, and you art students are preparing to paint murals on the moon.

So much for my education in the arts. Had it found me a way out? Was it feeding me?

One thing a fear of starvation does for you is that it inspires instant movement. I forced myself to forget I might start my wounds bleeding again and began to scoot back and forth the length of the bench top. I could not crawl on my knees because of the glass cuts on them, and the scuttling process got a few splinters in my bottom and the heels of my hands, but I searched with my brows nearly grazing the top of the workbench, fearful of overlooking some implement crucial to my survival.

With my nose so close to the bench, I noticed more than ever the smell of oil. I knew sometimes Larry did automobile and lawnmower repair things at this workbench. Motor oil had no doubt been spilled here and soaked into the unpainted wood. I sat up. My eyes opened wide and I began an hour-long search for a motor oil can opener. With that one tool, I could open the sealed inner lid of a jar of cherries. I could eat without worrying that I was ingesting glass. But, as the light was not very good, I crawled up and down, back and forth over the workbench for an hour feeling for and wishing with all my heart for a church key.

I found a few probably not useful items on the top of the workbench, but, otherwise came up empty. Shifting my attention to the bench's lower shelf, I squatted on my haunches to avoid scraping my sore knees, and duck-walked along the lower shelf. (Duck-walking is exhausting.) Running my hand across the thick oil-soaked and dust-draped planks in front of me, I crept up and down, back and forth for what seemed like an hour and found nothing more than patches of oil, a few nuts, and no bolt. If I had a nail, I thought, I could pound it through a jar lid with another jar, cap first. But Larry, in his infinite stinginess, had not provided me with a nail.

Not even one tiny screw--despite all my attempts to seduce you with my slinky robe, Larry.

I began to laugh at my pun, but had to stop or my starved body would have been found days later lying in the cellar dirt with the laugh still painted on its face.

My exploration of the dark space below the surface of the workbench did not reveal a crowbar or a thermos bottle filled with hot soup. All I picked up were some more nice fat splinters.

I did discover that there was a crawl space beneath the lower shelf–not for human crawling, but for mouse and beetle crawling–and I steeled myself to probe that unappealing area. There were dust kittens under there large enough to be called dust pumas, and I suspected the hair in them was not from kittens but from mice and rats and possibly moles.

I lay on the floor and tried to peer into the murk under the lower shelf of the workbench and ran my hand along its length right up against the cellar wall. The dirt wall was cold and damp and arrayed with hangings of spider web and roots. I often jerked my hand back, fearing that some poisonous species of spider had crawled all the way up from California to inhabit my cellar. Nothing bit me, but things explored my fingertips reciprocally, and I was certain there were things back there that wanted to nibble my fingers. I came across something metal stuck into the hard packed dirt of the wall behind the bench and, reaching my arm into the low dark space, I dug at it until I had loosened it sufficiently to pull it out with my pinky and my thumb. But, when I stuck my index finger into the hole I had made beside the object, I touched something that felt exactly like another finger. And it was moving.

Before it occurred to me that I had disturbed the home of a harmless earthworm, I had the strongest impression that I had come upon the probing finger of another abandoned housewife, trying to dig through the dirt wall separating our identical cells under Larry's and my house. Though it was stupid, I felt comforted for a split second in my solitude by the feel of the flesh of a fellow creature, if only the flesh of an earthworm. *And I'm sure not going to eat one of those.* If it had been a second wife my husband had stashed under the house, we could have been no help to one another anyway, beyond the comradery of two disregarded damsels. If there had been such a companion prisoner, she had not freed herself anyway, and was not likely able to help free me.

I pulled my finger back, and lunged back up onto the workbench, hugging my adventurous digit to my chest and protecting it with my other hand. After wiping earthworm residue off my finger with some newspaper, I prepared to examine the small store of items I had found by feel. Turning my back to the distracting jars of pears, peaches, plums, applesauce, berry jams and jellies, I re-crossed my legs on the workbench, pulled from my pocket my small cache of found thingamajigs and dumped them into my lap.

Intelligence Test No. 77. You are stranded on a desert island with only five items: a skate key, a hair pin, a roll of waxed paper, a can of sewing machine oil and a barrette. With only these items, design a device with which you can signal a passing rescue ship, survive until you are rescued, and cook a seven-course French dinner for a family of five.

Some genius from MIT could fashion an apparatus to escape from Mars with such homely items, but I had often mused that I could not have escaped from a large paper bag with all the tools they allow on those intelligence tests and a pair of gardening shears. And here were my only assets in my present situation: an eccentric ability to mark a scene with a mental grid, a high wooden bench, a tray, a thick stack of newspapers, a few items of hardware gleaned from the dirt and the bench (including a bobby pin that would turn out to be most useful), three broken Mason jars of jam with sealing caps and rings, the mood lighting produced by the ventilation window, and, encompassing all these treasures, a world of dirt.

Also among the few found treasures were a spark plug that had escaped Larry's cleansing ritual, one of my father's red handkerchiefs–chewed to lace at the edges by some unknown creatures–and a small spring, covered with dust like the rest of the items. The spring was of the sort that connects a flashlight bulb to the battery terminus. I wasted precious minutes stretching my arms underneath the lower workbench shelf again, sweeping them back and forth looking for the flashlight that must go with that spring. The batteries would no doubt have been dead by that time, but I was not thinking that clearly at the moment. There being nothing under the workbench but icky things inspiring ickier thoughts, I crawled back up onto the top shelf of the bench and gave way to feeling icky.

I also had one big fat nail. Could I pry up a sealed lid with its head? Might as well try. The fruit shelves were in a rough-hewn wooden bookcase ranging from ceiling to floor across the south wall of the cellar. I duck-walked across the workbench and, reaching out, grabbed a pint jar. Holding it between my knees and using the hem of my dress to grip the lid, I tried to unscrew it. It was a Kerr lid with the metal outer ring, and, even if I could unscrew it, I would still be faced with the flat metal middle cap and the rubber inner ring. I had screwed the lids on when they were still warm and, now, cold as a witch's tool kit, *(wish I had one)* they had contracted around the glass neck of the jar. Exactly the sort of jar lid I would have asked Larry to open if he had been here.

"Where are you when I need you, Larry?"

I had convinced him to tighten the ring caps on most of these jar lids. Why had I done that when I was the one who would have to unscrew them? And me without my rubber lid opener.

"When I get out of this, Larry, I swear, I will never ask you to open anything for me again." *Well, except for the cellar door.* "Because I will learn to open things myself."

Was there anything else in this hole that could serve as a surrogate lid opener? Ah, there was my apron lying on the bottom step where I had thrown it in anger all those eons ago before Larry evaporated. I scampered across the floor, grabbed it and hastened back to the workbench. The apron had a leatherette bodice, which proved to be a rotten substitute for the piece of rubber inner tube I used to open things in my kitchen. Wrapping the leatherette around the lid of the jar, I held it tight between my thighs and, gripping the lid with both hands, turned it with the determination of an underworld sprite cranking off the head of an evil gnome. Nothing. I tried wrapping the apron around both cap and bottom of the jar and twisted with both hands until I thought my brain would spring a leak from the effort, but the only movement that occurred was a spasm in my left thumb.

Inspiration! Though I regretted the loss of body fluids, I spit on the leatherette to make it gummy, and tried again. I twisted that cap so hard I feared I would sprain my fingers and be unable to do another thing to survive my predicament, but, after several alternating periods of effort and rest, I felt the ring-cap begin to give. With one final, extended twist, accompanied by an amount of grunting not usually heard from a member of the fairer sex, I unscrewed the outer ring! Then sat there looking at the implacably sealed inner cap.

The flat cap had been sealed--rubber between metal and glass–in a pressure cooker. Without the proper utensil, I could more easily separate conjoined twins than I could separate that cap from the jar. *What would those genius MIT guys do with my tiny armory of gadgets?* I felt around in my apron pocket for any other detritus I had plucked out of the dirt floor, but the only metal objects in there were the rusty bobby pin and my best power tool, the big nail. Sitting on the edge of the workbench, I tucked the jar between my thighs again. No way could I pry up the cap with the nail, but could I use it to poke a hole in the top? Grasping it in my good right hand like a small icepick, I brought the nail down as hard as I could on the jar lid. Missed the lid and stabbed my thigh. I jumped off the bench, tore a small pad of newspaper off the stack, lifted my skirt and dabbed at the bubble of blood growing out of my thigh. When the stain on the newspaper stopped increasing in diameter, I left a few sheets of the paper on the small wound to act as a Band-Aid while I continued my meal preparations.

If I can't poke a hole in the lid by jabbing at it with a nail, perhaps I can jab the nail with the jar lid.

I walked across the cellar to the doorpost, held the nail--point outward--against the wooden jamb with one hand, and, with the other, smashed the jar lid against the nail. The nail fell to the earth, the jar popped out of my hand and I very nearly failed to catch it before it fell to the ground and broke. Game over.

If I worked the nail up between two boards of the workbench, could I drop the jar onto the point hard enough to puncture the metal lid? *Gravity: Come to*

Mama! I rammed the jar onto the nail so hard the nail disappeared and I had to feel around on the lower shelf and then the disgusting dirt under it to relocate it.

Then a brilliant idea came into my head. I took Daddy's kerchief out of my apron pocket and pierced one corner of it with the nail. Then I folded over a bit of the kerchief and poked the nail through that as well. I did that over and over– folding and poking– until the nail could sit upright by itself on the workbench, firmly held in place by the pad of kerchief material. I brought the lid of the jar of fruit down on the nail with a gentle tap, then increased the force of the blows until I gave the nail one final whack with the lid. The jar slid sideways; the nail fell over onto its kerchief bed, and, despite a lengthy indentation across the lid's diameter, the cherries were as secure as ever in their glass enclosure.

Sweat was pouring down my face and between my breasts. Before I could even imagine trying to lift the sealed inner cap again, I had to rest. I lay back with my knees at the edge of the workbench and my lower legs dangling in midair. My eyes were closed and I tried to rest without thought while I gained energy for the next task. Imagine a man– imagine Larry– having to rest after opening a jar lid. *And after having a door slammed on him, don't forget, and hitting his head on the floor, as well as kneeling on glass shards, and being left like a sack of carrots to winter in the root cellar.*

I could see only one way out of my present dilemma, and that was a nap. Within seconds of lying back, I could not feel the grey planks under my back. I had been awake since well before dawn, and suddenly I could not have opened my eyelids any more than I could have opened the jar. A warm blankness was pressing into my entire body through my eyes, and, for all I knew, I no longer existed. Until the knocking began.

It was an insistent, sharp rapping as if on a tin drum. At first, sensing that awake was something I did not want to be, I tried to will away the tapping. In my mind, though, I leapt off the bench, while my body--stiff

of knee and sore of hip from napping in a damp hole--
was more reluctant.

"Who's there?" I cried, struggling to my feet at
last. "Larry? Is that you?" *And, if not Larry, who?* I
limped to the cellar steps calling, "Mama, Daddy?" I
called up the stairwell, "Who's that knocking!"

*That metal sound--as if the door is hollow. Can't
be the back door. They must be knocking on the metal
cellar door.*

Knock! Knock! Knock!

I pressed my cheek to the crack between the cellar
door and its frame, hoping to see a familiar face peering
back at me. Even the face of a stranger, a shoe salesman,
or a Jehovah's Witness would be a welcome sight.

Knock-knock. Knock-knock-knock!

"I'm here! Here! Who's there, dammit?"

The dialogue between me and the mystery guest
went on and on until I finally remembered the flicker.
One of the huge birds had taken a liking to the metal
drainpipe at the corner of the house outside Bertie's room
and used to peck on it until I would go outside and throw
a windfall pear at him. I never hit him, but it would send
him away long enough for Bertie to have his afternoon
nap. I could not at present get to the pears under the pear
trees outside, and the flicker might keep pecking until
sundown, incessantly, obsessively, madly. Why did he
do it? Did he think the drain pipe was a silver tree into
which he could peck a nest? It was not as wide as his
body and he never could have fit into it. Was he seeing
himself reflected in it and trying to kill a supposed rival,
or did he just love the sound of his own pecker?

Knock! Knock! Knock!

I spent a good hour of my life shouting at the bird,
pounding the underside of the cellar door with the side of
my fist and with jar lids, anything I could find. Knock!
Knock! Nothing I did threatened the flicker's territorial
pecking on my house.

I was going to go mad if I could not block out the
intrusive noise from the peace and quiet of my cloister.

"Do something useful, Flicker, and go find someone to help me out!"

Really, who else could come by and find me? Something about facing the impossible caused a sudden spurt of hope to rise in me. Someone besides my doting husband would surely discover my plight. The mailman came to mind, then went right out again. The post office would not send anyone all the way out River Road to deliver our mail, so we had a post office box in Salmon Run. Meter reader? I could not recall what part of the month the meter reader came by. Who else might drop by a remote farmhouse at the end of a dusty road? Any door-to-door salesman would find the distance between doors out here too daunting. Had we called a repairman lately–for the plumbing, the electrical wiring, the sump, the water pump? Should have, but no. Did we contract for any painters, floor refinishers, wallpaper hangers, tile setters, roofers, landscapers? *No, Kory, we did not call any workmen to do any work on our place at all, because you had to have your nine private days of artistic expression.*

We were such private people that not so much as an Avon lady visited our house more than once every generation. I might as well be a castaway on a remote island for all the traffic that was likely to approach within a mile of my house before Larry returned.

No one?

Knock, knock.

"I mean BESIDES the flicker! Oh, never mind."

Despite too few rescuers and too many noisy birds, I decided I would have to put off going mad for the present. I still had to find a way to feed myself.

Maybe the Fairies Did It

The flicker won the endurance contest. I fell asleep on the bench again with the sound of beak-on-tin poking at my head. He had stopped his racket by the time I woke. Or, maybe it was the cessation of the racket that awakened me. I lay languishing on my back on the workbench absorbing the pain of living without sound. Kind of missed the bird. Before I could meditate upon the idea that there could be a solitude so depressing one could be nostalgic for an unbearable din, an immense craving for food impressed itself upon me. When I opened my eyes to reapply myself to the task at hand, I was looking up at the rafters which support the floor of the house. The thought that Bertie's Big Boy Bed must be no more than a couple feet above my head made my throat swell with emotion. I glared murderously at the rafters under the floor lying between me and his bedroom--a domain of human comfort and love. At first, I was so absorbed with self-pity regarding my banished state that I did not notice that the crucial key to my survival was right in front of me.

The thing--furnished by the Fates or simple happenstance--was hanging from a nail which had been pounded into the side of one of the rafters. It shone dully in the light from the vent. At first, I was certain it was a bat suspended above me, and, although I have never been afraid of bats, I did not relish spending nine days in a cave-like setting with one. I squatted atop the workbench, and, after examining the thing closely enough to determine it was probably inanimate, I plucked the item from its support and threw it onto the workbench. To my surprise and near rapture, it was an old fashioned manual can opener, the kind with a rounded lever on one end and a triangular hole-poker on the other.

Larry would not have left even a cheap can opener to rust underground, so it had to be Daddy's, left from when he and my mother still lived in the house.

74

"Thank you Daddy, a million times!" I cried, clasping the can opener to my breast.

Examining its pointy, business end, I saw what looked like ancient sludge. Daddy must have kept a crate of oil for the car down here and used the can opener to open new cans as needed. Larry would not have noticed the opener hanging on the rafter above him, according to the rule that people do not look up unless a roman candle explodes directly above them. And can openers do not make much noise unless they are opening something fizzy.

Using the rounded end of the opener, I pried the inner lid off the pint of cherries. Carefully I slipped the inner lid and the rubber ring into the cap and began to eat. Nothing has ever tasted that good to anyone, anywhere, ever as that first sweet cherry tasted to me that early evening. The walls of the cellar melted away and I was sitting on the grass under the pear tree, rolling cherries like perfect spheres of ambrosia around in my mouth before chewing the flesh away from the pits and swallowing the fruits one by one. I sat on the edge of the workbench, swinging my legs to and fro like a kid on a fence and ate every last cherry in that pint jar. Then I sucked every shred of flesh off each pit. I did not want to leave any fruity pits out in the open to draw creepy creatures to my domain. Then I drank the cherry juice. I felt euphoric. I was still hungry, but it looked as if I was going to live.

I put the pits back in the jar and fit the lids back on it. I wanted to keep the slick of leftover sugary juice inside from drawing insects out of the niches and crevasses where they were biding their time till I fell asleep. *Now, where did I put the can opener?* I had a moment of panic. If I could not find that again, I could still starve in the days I might have left before I was found. I felt in my pocket but it was not there. I felt all over the workbench. Although I could not recall hanging the thing back on the nail where I had found it, I glanced up at the rafters, and there it was, just where I had found it in the first place. *I'm clever and methodical even when I don't know it. That must be a good sign for my survival.*

Energized by my success and the food, I did something I had been wanting to do since first I had found myself in this predicament. I climbed down off the workbench and made my way across the floor to the spot where the jam jars had broken. With my fingers, I tried to dig a hole in which to bury the jam from the broken jars, but the dirt floor was too hard packed from about a hundred years of stomping feet. One of the jars had broken cleanly away from its zinc lid and I was able to use it to scoop a shallow grave for the spilled jam. Maybe my efforts would not have exhausted me so completely, if I had not felt I was working against such overwhelming forces: the dark, the cellar walls pressing in on me, the imminent attack (I was certain) by vermin, and the loss of my freedom. After maybe an hour, I reckoned that I had buried the jam remains deep enough to discourage the tiny subterranean marauders who had appeared as if by parthenogenesis. I cleaned my hands as well as I could on a newspaper towel, rolled more of the newspapers into a cylindrical pillow, and fell worn-out onto the workbench.

After eating my first meal in what seemed weeks, I did not move right on to planning further necessary steps towards survival. While in the cellar, the reality of being imprisoned and abandoned hammered at me relentlessly except for when I was actively busy managing the basic functions of life. Having successfully completed the first challenge to my survival, therefore, I felt the immense weight of the cellar's earthen walls pressing in on me again. I climbed far into myself, wrapped a cloak of silence over my head, and claimed my customary refuge by daydreaming. In accordance with long habit, I sought the fantasy through which I regularly shut out unpleasant realities. Transforming regret into a mind-painting is what I called it. What did they call it in the medieval times? The *agayn bite of in wit.* The recurring pain of personal reevaluation. If only my family had encouraged my painting. If only I had insisted. Meanwhile, I had my mind-painting.

The nine years since I realized I was a painter is a long time, and in all that time why had I not found ways around the resistance my family, and especially Larry threw at me?

What did I do to you, Kory? After all, you chose me. You knew me when you married me.

I knew your summer face, Larry. I did not know your winter ways.

I would have sat there for nine days regretting my lack of resourcefulness or perception, if I had not felt a sudden breeze on my face. I had folded myself into the corner where the north cement foundation and the east dirt wall joined, therefore I knew it could not be coming from the north through the vent. It was a westerly wind and it was coming from the cracks around the door. I scrambled off the bench and ran to the stairs, heedless of creepy crawlers that might have poked their nasty noses out of the floor as the sun ran behind the bluff. I dove onto the cement steps and, rolling onto my back, lay with my nose as close to the crack in the door as it could get. Closing my eyes, I sucked at the breeze as a baby sucks milk. I could smell the juice of rotting pears which lay on the grassy verge of the driveway, gravel dust, freshly scythed grass, the musk of wasps and yellow jackets feasting on rotting fruit, and air, fresh air.

It was maddening to be able to smell freedom without enjoying it personally. *I am meant to be painting life right now, not regretting the way others have scheduled my life around them.* I opened my eyes and cursed at the dark door slanting over my face. Then I noticed something, a pink light glinting in the crack of the door. My heart nearly exploded with hope that someone had come for me. Someone with a pink flashlight?

"Hey!" I squeaked. "I'm here!"

I pounded on the door. Not as hard or as long as last time. My palms hurt too much.

"I'm here and I'm hurt!" I explained to the pink light. Then I realized what it was. The last of the sunset beyond the bluff was shining on clouds above, which directed the light downwards at the perfect angle to outline the shadow of the cellar door's hasp. The hasp should not have been lying across the door's opening, though. *Maybe when the door fell shut, the hasp slipped over the staple designed to hold the padlock?* That was not possible, was it? *Must be the hasp flipped onto the staple from the force of the door falling into place.* I thought that must have been what happened. It was not my weakness that had prevented my opening the door at least a crack: It was the hasp! All I would have to do would be to flip the hasp off of the staple. I would not need Larry's tool box to move a little flap of steel. I felt in my pocket for my big nail and stuck it up through the crack around the door. The door was so thick, though, that I could not reach the hasp with the tip of the nail. I began working it along back and forth in the crack between door and frame, looking for a spot wide enough for the nail to slip through all the way. Then I heard something.

Another car engine? Maybe Larry forgot something and came back for it.

"You forgot something, all right, Larry, and that something was your wife!"

I paused, listening, my nose to the crack under the latch. Just an airplane. If I had a little flag or a tiny search light, I could stick it through the crack and signal passing aircraft, I thought, and giggled. I was getting punchy again and I needed my wits about me. Did I even know Morse code for SOS? What a mess of misinformation I was.

I jerked upright so suddenly that I cracked my head on the cellar door.

My God! Larry may have realized he slammed the door, but he must not have looked back to see that the hasp had flipped into place.

Larry was always unsettled by something out of place. If he had misplaced his creel, or his rod, he would remember it somewhere down the road and come back for it. He would not go fishing with some reel he picked up at a sporting goods store on the other side of the Cascades. Larry put great value on what was his and on keeping it where it belonged. And, if he forgot it, he would remember it somewhere along the way and return for it. *He forgot his wife, but he'll remember and come back for her.*

After Larry had spent the first miles of his trip mulling over what we had said to one another before he left, he would remember having slammed the door--or that he had let it slam, or that it had slammed without his knowledge. But he would remember having heard the hasp clack into place. He would turn the pickup around with a cry of anguish on my behalf, making cascades of gravel spew off the shoulder into the deep canyon beside the highway. He would speed back to free me. Or, if it took him longer than usual to run his mental transcript and he found himself all the way on the other side of Mt. Hood when it happened, he would at least stop at a pay phone to call someone and ask them to check on me.

When he remembers what happened.

To calm myself, I reminded myself that I might have to wait until he had an ice chest full of fish or his nine day trip was over for my husband to get me out of this pickle. Unless someone else dropped by unannounced, I would have to poke the hasp off the staple by myself.

I felt in my pocket for the big nail again but did not find it. In my haste to alert what I had thought was a motorist arriving, I must have dropped it. I felt madly around me on the cement steps, in the folds of my dress and apron, in my pockets again. For such a large nail, it had an amazing ability to disappear between one moment and the next. Jack London's story *To Build a Fire* blew into my head like a fifty-degree below wind and filled me with panic. Had I, like that inept traveler in the Alaskan wastes, mishandled the one item that stood between me and a lonely death? The lone character in that story (if you do not count the wolves) dropped his matches in the snow, rendering them useless for building a fire, as I had dropped my big nail in a dirty cellar, rendering it useless to flip open the hasp of the door to my prison.

  Come on, Kory, it doesn't get that cold in Oregon.

  I smiled wryly at my melodramatic Jack London moment. Still, the clouds that had reflected the sunset down onto the hasp were the first clouds of August that year. Maybe the weather was changing. The temperature would not drop to fifty below, but it could drop enough to make sleeping in a dirt cellar uncomfortable. I continued my search for the big nail with renewed enthusiasm. I had to crawl down the steps and out onto the dirt floor, making broad sweeps with my palms before I found it imbedded in the dirt halfway out into the room. It must have dropped from my hand, bounced on a cement step, and I must have stepped on it. I had accumulated so many tiny wounds on my legs and feet in the past few hours, I would hardly have noticed it.

  I found a wide spot in the crevasse between door and frame and shoved the nail up through it as hard as I could. It slipped through with such an abrupt movement that I almost dropped it again in surprise. My fingers held it against the hasp above the door and, supporting the nail with the pit of my palm, I shoved it against the hasp as hard as I could. The hasp did not flip off of the staple. It did not even move it. I tried again and again. Using the zinc lid of a full fruit jar as a hammer, I punched the hasp with the nail until my upper arms felt like silly putty. Then I tried slipping one of the Kerr lids sideways through the crack. I banged it against the hasp for long minutes before admitting to myself I was unable to move the hasp.

Larry is right: I have let myself get way too weak for normal purposes.

But, was this situation normal?

Am I really that weak, or has somebody secured the arm of the padlock into place around the staple?

Of course not. No one locked up a spouse for arguing for the cause of the red huckleberry. Oh, all right, or for considering renting her land to an old friend to whom the family owed a big moral debt. "Hmm," I mused while idly punching the hasp with the nail, then the lid, then the nail again. "The tax quarter will lapse during the nine days Larry is gone. Part of the proposed agreement was that Nick would reimburse us for the property taxes. Nick had said that if he were to get his money's worth out of the tax payments, he would have to rent the land right when the next quarter began--to have the whole tax quarter to prepare the soil and to get the winter vegetable crop planted. Sure, Larry was touchy on the subject of Nicky, but would he lock me up to buy time until the next quarter? Would he?"

If there had been a light bulb hanging in the cellar, it would have clicked on at that point. *Someone locked me in.* I stared in horror at the shadow of the bolted hasp.

Not Larry!

Perhaps the fairies did it.

"Okay, maybe he did it! But not on purpose," I cried to my irritating alter ego. "He could have bolted the door out of habit when the cellar door fell shut," I protested to the worms and bugs, as I backed down the steps and stumbled backwards across the small underground room. Overwhelmed again with feelings of dread, loneliness and abandonment, I turned, collapsing over the work bench and sobbed on my forearms.

Don't do this!

I pushed myself upright as suddenly as I had collapsed. Even if I did not need to conserve water, I reminded myself, shedding tears during my marriage was exhausting. You would think it would be refreshing to purge yourself of grief and other desolate emotions by flushing all the teardrops out of your system. But I found myself so spent after a good cry that I became certain I had lost too much salt and had mortally affected the balance of my bodily chemicals. I remembered how all the crying I had done in the past few years had made the inside of my skull sting. The tissues of my face would get so soggy that I could feel my features sagging towards the floor. When I was in such a state, I was too weak and muggy-brained to do anything. Now, no matter whose fault it was that I was locked in the cellar, I had to stop crying. To do that, I would have to stop returning to the idea that my husband was going to rescue me.

If, on the other hand, I was going to figure a way out of the cellar by myself, I was going to have to be as strong and clear-headed as I ever had been. Stronger and clearer, probably. If escape was out of the question, I would have to find the source of my own survival in this cellar. Sadly, I did not think tears or the tiny cache of objects in my pocket would get me very far. On that note, I forced myself to stop crying. First time I ever did that. Personal progress gained the hard way.

Despite my resolve to be strong and rescue myself, as the daylight seeped out of the world, I did not at present have the strength left to struggle against the approaching dark. That was the ninth longest day of my life. There would be some after it that were even longer. Exhausted, I lay on my back staring up at the floorboards and beams under Bertie's bed. I could not even remember what Bertie's room above me looked like. Where was his dresser? Was the wind-up mobile he loved as a baby still hanging over his bed? I would have given anything to stand in the middle of his room and inhale his fragrance. I wished the molecules of my body could break into atoms and rise up between the atoms of the wooden ceiling and then recombine to make a new me–the sort of person who would never let herself get caught in her own damn cellar.

I was trying to think things through, but I was too weary from living at a primal level and from wracking my body and brain to understand why I was there and how to get free. If I could not stand this for a day, how had our cave-dwelling ancestors ever survived to carry on our race? And where was my primal memory of how to live underground? I lay there pretending I was a seer who could contact her cave ancestors, but, apparently, the primordial gift of inner sight had died out in my family before I was born.

Where is race memory when you need it?

Floating down the greasy spiral of ordinary memory, I imagined passing one crucial signpost of my life and heritage after another--so many memories passed with such speed that they blended together like one long curving billboard beside the highway of my life. I was unaware I was drifting into sleep even as I envisioned the naked slate of my ancestral memory.

When I awoke, it was dark and I had no idea where I was. I glanced around for guideposts that would tell me what room I was in, what house, what year. I could see that there was a small amount of light in the room. Following the light to its source at what passed for a window, I perceived the vertical bars of the grid and not the horizontal ones. I concluded I was in prison.

Innocent!

Not so innocent, dear Kory. You did lust after your neighbor, after all.

Hey! I lusted after my own husband first!

A lengthy internal inquisition followed, while I attempted to orient myself as to place.

Wo ist toilette?

As I often did when I awoke in my own bed with such an urge or when I was traveling in Europe the summer after college, I had lain for a moment trying to rouse myself enough to plan my route to the bathroom. With a start, I remembered where I was, and the dark crashed down on me again like a ton of dirt. I had rather been in prison. They feed you there. They put a bucket in your cell. But, the angle of the light in my cell had altered drastically telling me the sun had moved way beyond the canopy of the trees on the bluff. Night was coming on and it was going to be darker and colder, I was willing to bet, than in most jails.

My impulse was to seize the opportunity of last light to scurry around and do all the little things that must be done before dark. As twilight threatened on an ordinary day, I would take out the trash, turn off the lawn sprinkler, rinse my hands, pick a fresh pear from one of the backyard trees, eat it while admiring Mt. Hood's snowy pink facade from the side yard, take in the hand laundry from the clothesline beyond the twin pear trees, or rake up the grass in the meadow Larry had scythed the day before. And, though the light was still bright enough in the yard and the house for the many final tasks I could have done if I were above ground, the rays were crippled by the time they made it through the tiny cellar vent. A feeling of discomfort reminded me that what I wanted to do before the sun left my house on this day was to use the toilet.

Swiftly, I conducted a review of my bathroom options. I did not relish leaving my relatively bug-free platform, but I really had to go. First I cowered on the workbench, imagining I heard platoons and divisions of bugs scavenging for edibles all over the cellar walls, floor and ceiling. I felt an itch on my back, on my elbow, my foot. When I slapped the itches I felt no tiny bug bodies, but I was suspicious about them all the same. The cherries had gone through me like a bullet through buttermilk, and I did not have the time to dig a hole to pee in with my Mason jar lid. There was nothing else for it, the cherries would have to go back to the place from whence they had come.

I fumbled around until I found the empty jar on the under shelf of the bench, took a handful of newspapers and, laying down stepping stones of newsprint in front of me from the bench to the far corner of the cellar, I opened the cherry jar and put it to good use. That was one jar that would never be part of the canning process again. When I had completed the cycle of Nature, and cleaned myself with newspaper, I screwed the lid on tight again, set it up against the wall farthest from my bench bed, scoured my hands with dirt, retraced my steps via my newspaper stepping stones, and sanitized my hands with fresh newsprint,

I lay back down on the top of the workbench, pulled my apron up over my shoulders against the cool of the oncoming evening and tried to go back to sleep. I supposed I could survive thus for a time, but at that moment, I conceived of or discovered in myself a reverence for water as the most sacred thing in creation. I would have devoted the rest of my life to good works for one quart of the stuff. Or, just enough to wash my hands properly. And, a mouthful to rinse my teeth. I tried to recall what water was like, slippery when I floated on an inner-tube down the Silky as a teenager, so cold it stung hard when my bottom bumped against the rocks of the rapids. The taste of the water of the Silky up in the watershed, above the places where men live and dump things into the river. Warm, lapping against me, soaking my hair as I lay on the sandy bottom of a pool at the foot of our lane. I floated in water until I thought I could drink the whole river and still not be quenched. But the memory of water had the opposite effect from the real stuff, I found.

Memory is an overrated function. Memory is....

I sat up so fast, I almost hit my head on the floorboards of Bertie's room.

What if someone had come by and purposely locked me in? The way Mama did that time.

Fur Coats and Green Olives

"Daddy, help me!   Someone's locked me in again."

Why wouldn't he help me? He freed me that other time.

After thinking someone who loved me might have betrayed me, my first thought was that my father could save me. Historically, he was, after all, my rescuer.

I was four, and had already become a sneak by that age: Whenever I saw Mama sitting at the kitchen table eating green olives all day waiting for Daddy to come home for dinner, I knew I should disappear from view. At the age of four, I could turn the back door knob and get out of the house on my own. Or, quick as a skittering cricket, I would crawl out the dog door or find a low window open–any aperture where I might escape my mother's deadening loneliness. At the age of four, the smell of green olives was reason enough to send me creeping up the backyard bluff to smell a fresh breeze.

The first day I climbed the bluff Mama was slumped at the kitchen table as if a great hand had reached in through the chimney and submerged her body in invisible glop. I asked her if there was anything I could do to help her feel better. She slapped my face, and then threw her head on her arms and cried as if I had slapped her. At that age, I did not know what causes depression, but I soon learned to stay away from it.

No way past Mama and out through the kitchen that dreadful day though. I tried the doggie door but Daddy had nailed it shut after he accidentally ran over my dog. In a panic, I scampered through the house looking for open windows, but they were all locked with those revolving clasps that my four-year old fingers could not budge. The hall closet door was ajar and, desperate to get away from the pall that emanated from my present-yet-absent mother, I twisted the doorknob, slipped into the closet and closed the door.

At that time, I still loved the closet. It held the prime aromas of our family: the engine oil fragrance on the jacket Daddy wore when he changed his motor oil, my good Easter coat that still smelled like marshmallow peeps and tiny candy eggs, and, best of all, my mother's fur coat, which smelled like her perfume. That coat held all of what was best in my mother. Because she wore it when she was happily on her way to some special occasion with Daddy, I thought of it as the furry skin of my other mother, the one who was sparkly and smiley. I plunged into it and wrapped its welcoming folds around me. While I was in the closet, luxuriating in my solitude amid some slaughtered creatures' fur, I stroked the sleeves and lapels of the faux epidermis of my mother. Feeling sad for the animals who had been murdered for their skins, I wondered what they had been like when they breathed and caught mice or whatever it was they did for a living.

Rubbing my cheek absent-mindedly against the coat, I poked around in its satin pockets and found some coins. And I deserved them, too. My mother had slapped me. What did a woman too distracted from her child-rearing duties by her novels, her green olives, her projects and her naps need with a few coins? I extracted from her pocket a dime, two nickels and three pennies, which I identified by their size and the ridges or lack of ridges on their edges. I dropped them one by one into the rick-rack bordered pocket of my pinafore.

The way I felt then–good girls who care about their virginity must feel that way when they lose it–was condemned. A conscientious person who has let down her moral guard just long enough to steal from her mother knows that all the rest of the zillions of seconds of her life she will know herself to be a very bad girl. That is how I felt after I purposely dropped Mama's change into my pocket. When one day I tottered up to the great golden throne, God would close his eyes and pretend I was not there. Jesus would refuse to shake hands with me, preferring to turn aside and bathe a scabby leper's crumbling feet. St. Peter would not have let me into heaven in the first place, but, sneak that I was, I would have squeezed in through the bars of the pearly gates. In Sunday-school pamphlet images, my dreadful future spread out before me. Stealing from my mother was the first step into what I--in my Sunday-school-titillated conscience–feared was to be a long and dreadful life of crime.

Having endured a four-year-old's agonized reflection about sin, I knew I had to run to Mama and confess what I had done. I would tell it as a joke at first, but, if that did not move her, I would plunk each of her coins on the table before her and howl for her forgiveness. I believed money left lying around not in anybody's piggy bank, purse or wallet was up for grabs, just as money found in the gutter belonged to the first person who found it, but I was pretty certain that is not what the world would believe when it discovered my secret life of crime.

Anxious to begin the atonement process, I disengaged myself from the furry body of the coat and eagerly reached for the knob of the closet door, ready to run as fast as I could to my mama and confess my crime. Only, there was no knob on the inside of the door. There was only a wing nut. It had been easy enough to slip my fingers around it in order to pull the door shut, but I could not get a grip on it to open it again. And, if I had been able to grab it firmly, I still would not have had enough strength to turn the crescent doohickey. What kind of a cheapskate family does not spring for a knob for the inside of a door as well as the outside?

I was stuck. And it was dark in there. Our closet was not adjacent to an outside wall and so did not have one of those small jewel windows. What was the matter with my family that it did not have a jewel closet window? The dark that had happily concealed me from my mother became disgusting to me the moment I realized I was stuck in it. I could feel the murk of the darkness all over me like heavy blankets of tiny vermin, vicious and hungry to devour me. Linked together arm-in-arm, their feelers twining to form a solid swath of insect-fabric, they crawled and breathed all over me with their suffocating bug-breath.

Mama! I called, in my I-got-myself-in-trouble-and-I'm-ashamed voice.

No response.

I squatted down and put my mouth to the slit underneath the door and called again, louder this time. Even with my face at the aperture between door and jamb, I could see no light. I stuck my finger down there, but discovered that there was weather-stripping to keep the cool of the closet from infecting the warmth of the house. I did not know at the time what weather-stripping was, but I knew it would probably prevent anyone from hearing my call for help. When I grew up, my house would have closets made of glass. They would have holes in the doors where you could yell for help if you got stuck in them. Every closet would have a back door. Maybe ours had one. I pushed through the heavy mass of coats to the side wall of the closet, and, crying for my mama, made my way by feel all the way around back to that unyielding door. When my fingers brushed that fragmentary knob again, I started yelling in earnest. I howled for help. I called Mama by every name I could think of. I even remembered her maiden name and called her by that. *Mildred Dohr. Mildred Dohr!* Then, suddenly, I became quiet.

What if she had meant me to be in here? What if she had slapped me and now sat unresponsive and glum at the table on purpose so that I would look for solace in the closet? What if she had been trying to poison me for years but had not been successful and, in desperation, had taken the inside knob off the hall door and had tricked me into the closet? Every horrible possibility known to the four-year old imagination went through my head and was exaggerated in the horror of that dark place.

Meanwhile, my mother, absorbed in her usual daytime activities of silently fretting, napping, reading novels and sucking the pimento strips out of green olives, did not hear me, or refused to hear me–I did not know which. By the time Daddy came home, I was sleeping fitfully, huddled in a back corner of the closet, my mother's fur coat wrapped around me. When the door opened and he hung his jacket on the rod above me, I woke with a scream, and sprang towards the light. Pushing past my father, I was out the open front door like a kitten who has been shut in a dresser drawer for a week. And, I kept running.

Now, recalling how I had felt squeezed into a small fur ball in the back of the hall closet, I felt the dirt walls of the cellar closing in on me as if they had not already been just about as close as they could get. I longed for the feeling I had experienced when Daddy freed me from the closet. I had run around the house to the backyard and climbed the cliff behind it before my father had recovered his surprise and descended the front steps calling for me. I had squeezed into the shallow cave behind the Kissing Boulders to hide from Mama before, and, I suppose I planned to hunker there in the dark until my life of crime faded from everyone's minds.

There was too much closet-like dark behind the Kissing Boulders, though, and I scrambled up the dogwood tree on the cliff side behind the rocks for some fresh air and a glimpse of sky. The tree was in full leaf at that time of year, and I climbed higher seeking the more scantily clad branches. Then I saw the ledge, and, without stopping to think how I would get back down the bluff, I crept out to the thin part of a branch and let it lower me down to the ledge. Clinging to roots and brush sticking out from the cliff wall, I scooted around past the dogwood branches and, clasping a red huckleberry bush that grew out of a tree stump rooted right in the cliff wall, I turned east to breathe in the early evening air. I could just see the tip of Mt. Hood sticking up above our house. Still, I needed to see more sky. The house, with all its closets and dark nooks and crannies, was always getting in the way of the sky. Grabbing a large tree root above me, I pulled myself upwards and away from the house. I found another ledge, a root, a smooth dirt lane. That was the first time I realized there was a narrow trail, snaking back and forth across the bluff's face.

In the cellar, recalling that climb, I remembered that it felt like climbing Mt. Hood, it took me so long. When at last I reached the top, I lay panting, and Daddy's call from the foot of the bluff sounded thin as a mewing kitten's. I could see him and Mama combing the meadow for me. I curled up on a flat boulder that rose above a fringe of golden grasses. I took deep breaths, trying to suck in the whole liberating sky. I could imagine nothing less like a dark closet than that spot, and I felt such relief. I just lay there and smiled at the sky as if it were my true parent.

When the sky began to turn pink, I began to worry. Soon it would be dark, and being up here with all that dark sky would be like being in Night's coat closet. I began to long for my *"Time to Retire"* night light with the sleepy blond kid holding a candle with one hand and a huge tire with the other. I would have climbed down earlier, but thought I would get much more than a slap for thieving and then running away. By the time the pink had been replaced by cold grey, I wished I had chanced it earlier and gone home. Too late. I could see a police car and fire engine coming down River Road, with lights flashing and sirens howling. If I went back down the bluff, I would be taken to jail. I thought of the 23¢ in my pinafore pocket and began to sob into my apron.

Even if I had not been certain my crime had caught up to me, it was too dark by then for me to find my way down the cliff, so I took off through the wild grass atop the bluff in search of civilization. Once when I had been up in the quarry behind our house with my daddy, he had told me the humming sound we heard up there was a road with cars and tractors. Maybe someone in a car on that road or on a tractor in the field could drive me home to face the music. If another adult was with me, I reasoned, my mama would not slap me as hard.

After stumbling through briar and burr, I arrived, finally, at the back door of Farmer Nakamura's house. His wife took me in, washed and band-aided the worst of my scratches while Mr. Nakamura coaxed my daddy's name out of me. Meanwhile a curious little face with huge black eyes peered at me around the corner. That was my first meeting with Nicky. While I drank a cup of cocoa loaded with marshmallows of thrilling rainbow colors, Mr. Nakamura called my parents to come get me and take me home.

"What happened?" my daddy implored.

"I went for a walk and got losted," I said, lying my larcenous little tongue off.

"Don't you ever do that again," warned my mother. "We thought you'd gone into the old orchard."

"I called and called you, Mama," I explained to her, my lip quivering, "But you wouldn't hear me."

"Who knows, I might have heard you," she whispered, bending down to pull up my anklets. "You're always scaring me to death, running off and playing hide and seek. It might have done you good to stew in your own juice for a while."

With that, my mother yanked the floor from beneath my feet, and I was falling through space in an unfamiliar neighborhood of the universe. I reached out to my father to catch me before I hit bottom so far away he would not be able to reach me ever again.

"Remember, you're my Sparkle Plenty," Daddy reminded me, giving my shoulders a brisk shake. "You're as strong as any boy," he whispered to me when we got home, while he fed me crackers crushed in a glass of warm milk and then tucked me into bed.

Huddled in the corner of the cellar workbench, I remembered how close I had felt to my father at that moment. I had cried with such relief to be saved. Until he put the cap on my adventure.

92

"After this, remember, you can't go running off. It's your job to stay home and look after your mama," he had enjoined me.

He turned on my *"Time to Retire"* night light, blew me a kiss and left the room. I lay in bed, weighed down by the task he had laid on me as if it were a lead comforter, and cried sad, angry tears.

Remembering, in the cellar, I cried again, reliving the suffocating feeling of having my father give me a job which confined me in a small house with a depressed pimento eater.

Now, imprisoned with my memories, I cried until my eyes felt as if hot sponges were lodged in them, the bridge of my nose was about to explode off my face, and my teeth ached. Strange, but I almost welcomed the pain when it replaced my memories. The aching formed a buffer between me and that empty room, between me and betrayal, between me and fear. I was not brave enough to embrace pain for very long, however, and, to escape its unrelenting regard, I fell asleep.

My own feet kicking the dirt wall next to the workbench disturbed my repose. Something was trying to break through the dual shields of pain and sleep.

Hi, Kory, wake up if you're asleep.

No. The earth's too heavy on my lids for me to open them.

Kory!

With a start, I jerked upright on the workbench. An actual sound had wakened me.

Kory!

It had to be a dream. But, after the voice stopped crying my name, the sound of a motor.

Larry?

I jumped up and moved to the ventilation grill as if the earthen wall behind me had taken a bite out of my flesh. As I leapt, my mind moved from dozy to crystal clear in a millisecond.

There is some light coming in the grill. I have slept through the night. A whole day in the cellar. So far.

I screeched my husband's name.

Larry!

Then I waited to hear the brakes squeal, gravel spatter against the cellar door, the motor stop, the car door fly open. But the sound of the motor was not coming closer. It was fading away. And it was not Larry's big new pickup. It was my father's battered old Ford. I recognized the ping, ping, ping of the pickup truck which my father was too cheap to have fixed. Daddy believed in using his spark plugs until they had not another spark in them.

I stood on the workbench and smashed my face against the wire grating of the vent, screaming every variation on the word Help! I could think of.

SOS! Save me! Firemen, Firemen! The grass around the trash bin caught fire again!

Not a familiar siren to be heard.

Mama, I'm having a nightmare!

I've fallen out of an apple tree in the orchard!

Rape! (I only shouted that once, realizing Daddy would run in the other direction if he heard that.)

Murder! Mayhem! I'm drowning!

I kept it up until Daddy could not have heard me screaming unless he had been hunkered down right outside the air vent. My voice, which had returned with rest, had worn out again. The motor had burped and sighed its way down the drive, turned onto River Road, and made its noisy way back towards my parents' new house.

Why did I decree a nine-day ban on my parents' coming to the house they gave me?

The answer to that was easy. The greatest drawback of living so close to my parents was a classic one. My folks dropped by almost daily with the slimmest of excuses. Though both my parents took some silent pride in my artistic accomplishments, they did not understand my need for solitude while I was painting. Daddy would drop by to remind me, for example, that the pump house needed to be kept closed during the winter so the well pump would not freeze. In mid-July Daddy had scurried over to remind me of that. I had been elbow deep in Titian red at the moment, brushing just the right color onto the highlight on a dewdrop sliding down a current berry at dawn. Then he asked if the coffee was hot and sat down for a nice chat while the colors on my current berries sagged, along with my inspiration to finish that painting in time to air out the house before Larry got home from work. Today Daddy had perhaps come by to tell me the grass in my meadow had turned gold and that we ought to have it mowed? No, he told me that last week. He was the kind of dad who might tell me again though. *Have we cut the golden grasses of the south field yet?* Remembering day before yesterday was getting difficult...remembering my own name was not as easy as it used to be either. *Yes, Larry scythed the grass. My memory is not gone. It's just slower than it was.*

As my parents were nosiness personified, it was not difficult to think they might ignore my request that they leave me alone for nine days. I had done everything but throw myself on the floor and hold my breath until I turned blue to convince them I really needed time alone to work on the paintings for my gallery show. Trying to put five miles between me and them, however, had been like trying to extricate myself from quicksand. Surely they would not be able to leave town without dropping by to offer me one more dollop of advice about being a normal wife, mother and steward of the family homestead.

But, as the ping of Daddy's pick-up dwindled away, I knew he was probably driving back home to finish packing up the car for their clam-digging vacation. Tomorrow, he would pack up Mama and Bertie in the sedan and take off for the beach.

"Stubborn old man!" I squawked out the vent. "You wouldn't get a hearing aid when the doctor removed the tiny bones in your inner ear. I am dying of your vanity." My voice had diminished to a stage whisper by then, and the pinging of the motor and the crunching of pickup tires on gravel had long since dwindled into the distance.

What was so important that he had come to ask me or to tell me before they left on their trip anyway? The day before had been my first whole day without Bertie since his birth, and I had the usual misgivings of a mother letting her child out of her sight for his first extended visit away from home. Was Bertie okay? I pressed my face up against the window grill as if I could see the color of my father's reason for contacting me wafting on the wind. Nothing but the dust Daddy's truck had kicked up on River Road settling on the leaves of the orchard.

Whatever the reason for his visit, he had certainly given up easily. He may have accidentally freed me from the closet way back when, but, aside from that, he and my mother did not have a good record of rescuing me from distress.

Just a couple years earlier I had tried to engage them in a discussion about my unhappy marriage, whereupon they had claimed family dysfunction to be a phenomenon utterly foreign to their sphere of knowledge. As adamantly as my mother had protected me from harm by keeping me from social situations outside the home, she was not going to ally herself with me against my husband even if he tied rocks to my body and threw me in the Silky to drown. My husband had never hit me, of course, but, when I was pregnant with Bertie, Larry had accidentally left his prints on my upper arms when he forced me into the car for flirting (he claimed) with a gas station attendant. I had called Mama and Daddy from back east and asked them to send me money or a ticket so I could come home.

"What did you do to cause him to bruise your arms?" Daddy asked.

"I asked the guy who was pumping our gas, *How goes it?*"

"You smile at people too much," Larry had said.

"Must have been more to it than 'How goes it?'" Daddy murmured.

"And, I can just imagine what you said to Larry," Mama huffed. "I have always suspected this honesty business you young couples indulge in. Use some wifely tact, for goodness sake."

"All I said to him was that I wasn't flirting with the guy in greasy overalls, Mama."

"Don't say anything. Just get in the car next time. You'd think you were brought up by rodeo people," Mama declared.

"Why, are rodeo people pathologically friendly?"

"No, they're too stubborn to put the horse in the barn when it starts to rain."

"Do you think I'm too friendly, Mama?"

"What I think is beside the point."

"I've always told her that," Daddy bragged.

I had to laugh.

Then I cried, and they hung up. Mama was always great when I was physically at risk from germs, tainted food or natural disasters, but emotions intense enough to cause tears were a threat neither she nor Daddy felt strong enough to withstand.

To their credit, they did not turn away from me completely. Though they did not send me a ticket or the money for a ticket, they sent an affectionate letter to Larry promising to give their house to me if we moved back to Salmon Run when we finished graduate school. Not really responsive to my needs, but, at least Mama and Daddy's generous gift proved to me they were aware on some level that some response to my plea was necessary.

Now, my parents' flaws seemed to be my only hope: they were fussbudgets and would surely find something to fuss about before the sun set on my predicament. Even though I had stormed and fretted until they promised they would let me alone for nine days, it was impossible to think of my parents minding their own business for all that time.

Looked at one way, my father had come to rescue me minutes ago--although he had probably not known that was what he was doing. It was I who had missed him. My anger drained away when I acknowledged to myself that, my father had not failed me. I was the one who had failed to be saved.

Too late, Kory. You missed your chance.

"It's never too late!" I cried aloud. There was always a chance my mother might come through at last.

Painting by ESP

When I was a child and I had my nightmare of the monster in the riverbank, Mama would come to my bed and lay beside me until I went back to sleep. Awake, she had no lap, but she had a perfect horizontal lap while sleeping spoons. I could never ascertain the temperature of my mother's heart, but her body curving around mine in bed after a bad dream was the perfect temperature to comfort a little girl. In case I had one of my nightmares, my bedroom door was open all night, and sometimes when Mama and Daddy would stay up late talking in the kitchen at the other end of the house, I could hear them raise their voices. One night I clearly heard danger in my mother's voice.

"The scamps see those apples hanging across the river from them and–just imagine how ruby red they look and how delicious they must seem to one of those poor creatures."

"Doesn't matter how scrumptious they look," my father said. "Those apples are ours."

"The apples are all wormy now anyway," I could hear my mother whisper loudly to my father. "Let's bulldoze the lot of them and prevent a tragedy."

"Those trees are our only windbreak from the east wind," Daddy would counter. "Take them away and the dust from the farmlands across the river will blow into this house and cover everything like powdered sugar on a dirt cake."

"I'll tape the seams around the windows and doors."

"That won't do any good. That east wind could shoot confetti through a brick wall. This is an old house and it has tiny seams in it you can't see, though the wind can."

"Then fill in the scamps," I thought Mama whispered. It was years before I would realize she had said, "Fill in the swamps."

99

"Do you know how much all that would cost?" Daddy asked.

"One day one of them will swim across and venture up towards the orchard," she countered. "But he won't make it because he'll come to that terrible place and be consumed."

Consumed by the beast in the riverbank?

"They'll be all right," Daddy soothed.

"Put up a warning sign at least."

"You know what the lawyer said," Daddy whispered. The muffled urgency in his voice terrified me.

I rolled back my covers and tiptoed to my bedroom door to hear what it was the lawyer had said. *Beware of Monster!* That's what I guessed Mama's sign would say.

"If we don't put up a sign, we will be at fault, when it happens," Mama said.

"If we issue a warning, we will be legally liable," Daddy corrected her.

"We will be morally at fault if we don't," Mama concluded.

"Or, we will lose our property in order to pay for a suit brought by those little meddlers' tribe." Daddy's voice had rung its final note and Mama had no answer for that.

When they married, Daddy had given up his right to fish and golf with his buddies and Mama had given up her right to deal with the world outside the home. That was their pact, and, if Mama wanted Daddy to be with her every moment he was not working, she had to keep her part of the bargain. My part was to creep back to bed and dream about the Scamps monster, tortured and dangerous in its sand cave.

Because I was prohibited from going to the river through the apple trees, I did not come face to face with the menace hidden between the orchard on the west and the mass of blackberry vines on the south–not when I was a child. It was not until much later in my life that I discovered Mama was not so much trying to protect our property from the scamps, as to protect the scamps from our property. For, as I would later find, the riverbank was not steep at the foot of the orchard, as I had dreamed, but low, flat, and very wet. Whether the scamps were Native American children, a monster in the riverbank or any other threat to my wellbeing as a child, my mother could turn overprotective at the blink of an eye. Now when I needed her to open the cellar door, it was past time for her overprotective side to turn golden. I had better not sleep at all.

I was lying in a crumpled womb position on the cellar workbench straining for the sound of my mother's voice when the phone upstairs rang again. I jumped all the way off the bench.

"Mama?"

It struck me that when Daddy had arrived back home yesterday, Mama would have interrogated him, as was her custom. I could just imagine their dialogue:

"Is Kory all right?"

"Don't know. She didn't show."

"So, you don't know if she's alive or dead."

"I assume she's alive."

"But she didn't answer the door?"

"I knocked a couple times, but she told us not to disturb her."

"But, as long as you were there–as long as you had to stop by anyway–I'd call that a loophole, wouldn't you?"

"I don't think Kory intended there to be any loopholes this time. She might have just touched her brush to the canvas the minute I drove up. I didn't want to take the chance."

"Her first night alone since--well, since never. Before we drive to the beach, we ought to make sure she's all right."

"I've still got to finish packing the car. You give her a call. Maybe she's gone shopping for a tube of toilet-white oil paint or something. We don't want to drive all the way up the road again for nothing."

The phone rang ten times before it stopped. That had to be my mother. But, would she succumb to her characteristic inclination to come by and interrupt my day just to make sure I had not fallen down the well?

"I did fall down the well, Mama! Since I didn't answer the phone, you have to know I'm not all right."

I sat with my face pressed against the grill of the vent watching for my snoopy mother to gallop to my rescue. Minutes went by. In my mind, I traced my parents' process as they climbed into the packed car, backed out of the driveway, and turned upriver towards my house. They would park in the driveway, walk around to the south lawn to peek in the sunroom windows to see if I was painting, and, not finding me there, they would knock on the door. Not obtaining an answer, they would search the property with hounds and dragnets if necessary. They would find me. But, too many minutes had gone by for that simple drive down River Road. Bertie must have had to take a last-minute bathroom break. Or, maybe they called the phone company to see if my phone was in service. There were so many things that could have slowed them down. As each new impediment popped into my head, I mind-traced their drive from their house to mine again. The theory in such cases is that, if you imagine it in realistic detail, it has to happen. Still, they did not come.

"All those years of anxious intrusion and where are you now, Mama?"

Surely she would come and at least peer in the windows to check on my safety. It was not as if my mother had never smashed her features against one of my windows to see where I was hiding from an unwanted visit.

There was still time, though. Mama and Daddy were not to start for the beach with Bertie until Monday. That would give them this evening and very early tomorrow morning to realize they had better check on me. The most likely thing that would get Mama to show up at my door this week would be a panic attack about some perfectly normal five-year old thing Bertie did or said. My spirits rose when I imagined how it would be. She would burst through my door spouting endless questions about the care and feeding of Bertie:

"Is it all right if we give him a sugary cereal just one time? His little forehead gets all sweaty when he plays in the sandbox. Do little boys sweat, normally? You never did that. Or, is he feverish? He won't eat his dinner. We can't get him to go to sleep. He pouts so much. You never did that. What is wrong with him?"

Usually when Bertie was at their house, she would call me every twenty minutes or so to ask how to solve every preschooler's problem from: *How do we get him to eat his greens?* To*: Why does he keep asking questions all the time?*

"Why do *you*?" I once replied.

"Why do I what?"

"There you go again, Mama."

To my credit, I fell short of wishing Bertie would scrape his knee or actually hurt himself in some way so that my mother would come by to get a Captain Kangaroo Band-Aid and to complain for the umpteenth time how much more trouble boys were to care for than her girl had been. (She had conveniently forgotten how many times I had run away in my youth and had been brought home again with an alarming new bruise or scrape.) But I did wish Bertie would become homesick or have some other minor concern that only a mother could soothe.

Only a few waking hours until they would leave for the beach.

Stay awake, Kory. Stay awake. Stay awake. Focus on Mama.

"Why, oh, why couldn't I have inherited the psychic powers my mother claims she has?"

I had always disdained Mama's claims that she had ESP where I am concerned.

"Get out of my head, Mama," I would laugh. "My thoughts are private, and invading the thoughts of an artist borders on plagiarism." Mama paid me no mind. After I left for college, she had continued to strain her brain to see what was going on in mine. From my freshman year right through graduate school, she had Daddy dial me regularly during the phone company's low-rate time period. She would wake me from a sound sleep to ask me with a quivering voice if I was all right.

"I'm okay. Why do you ask?"

"I had one of my feelings," Mama would say.

"What feelings?"

"You know–about you. Like you'd fallen into a pit or something."

"Not too many pits in my neighborhood, Mama. It's wall-to-wall sidewalks and parking lots." *I knew so little about pits, it turns out.*

"Don't be smart. Are you depressed?"

At that time, I had not yet begun to suspect that Mama called me whenever she was especially depressed, projecting the feeling across the country at me in that daughter-as-mirror way she had.

"A certain level of depression is required of all graduate students, Mama."

"That's ridiculous. I brought you up to be happy."

Really? How did I miss that?

Even though I could reason away Mama's ESP as a projection of her own feelings, it always gave me the willies when she called to ask if I was depressed when, as it happened, I really was depressed. One of those times occurred the first time Larry disparaged one of my paintings. Our typical grad school existence could be depressing enough without that. On most days, I was just able to hold it all together as a graduate student–cooking Larry's meals and serving them on our tiny drop-leaf wooden table with the chipped pea-green paint, and obsessively mopping the floors of the apartment--which, if the linoleum had been an ocean, the tide was definitely going out, revealing beneath, instead of sand, a beach of rotting particle board. Larry said we had money enough for only one study lamp, so we had to study with our desks jammed up against one another with the light almost in the middle between them (more on his side, because, he said, his studies were more academic). I wrote my fanciful (my professor said) essays for Art Appreciation class, comparing the lustrous reproductions of famous paintings in the books I borrowed from the university library and spread across my desk in the half-shade before me. I did come up with some imaginative interpretations of art: seeing them so poorly, I had to make up most of what I saw. I expect going through that process night after night for two years might account for the praise one of my professors gave for one of my paintings. *How did you achieve this wonderful infusion of light?* If any struggling art students someday had to study my paintings in inadequate light, I wanted my images to provide light unavailable in nature, I explained to him. When Larry looked at the painting and read my professor's comments, he laughed.

"I'll tell you where you can put your wonderful infusion of light. It'll do more good there than in your weird paintings."

I loved Larry more than I had ever loved another adult, but it was difficult to become the most famous artist Salmon Run ever produced while living with a man who held the depressing view that his wife had been formed from one of his ribs by some heavenly technician who had muffed the process. And, whenever Mama's avowed ESP caught me in a depression, I had to face the bleakness of trying to be creative on an ill-lit chipped pea-green table. At those times, it would take me days to reclaim my habit of shining the light of imagination into the dark places of my life.

Confined now in a cellar, with no infusion of light, how ironic to be wishing that Mama was at that moment having one of her previously unwelcome mother-daughter ESP moments.

Your vaunted clairvoyance on me had better not be out of service today, Mama.

No harm in testing her abilities, anyway. But, how to draw my mother's thoughts to my present misery? To my knowledge, I had no talent for ESP. I only had one mental talent, planning paintings in my mind when I was unable to get to my easel and brushes. Kept from my easel by a sturdy cellar door, I decided I could be redeemed by mind-painting again. A dab of red there, a set of sweeps of cornflower brushed on over there had saved me and would save me again. First, the architecture of the image sketched in thin grey lines. Now to attract the light into the picture, and then to focus the eye of the watcher. Finding the mythological figure. Was he, she or it imbedded in that stone? Hidden in cloud? Curled around a dust demon? I decided, I would mind-paint my dilemma so well that I could send it to my mother via ESP. To one confined against her will in a hole in the ground without ready means of escaping, this idea did not seem half bad.

"In my mind, I am painting you a picture of a lady in a hole, Mama," I said to the dark spot in the room where I wished she were standing. "I enter the sunroom, open the easel, and assemble my paints and brushes. The paintings are as clear in my mind as the memory of my son's face lit by the candles on his fifth birthday cake."

That day I painted for my mother many mind-paintings of my current situation as a woman entrapped in a hole filled with dark. I painted the Hellenic maiden Danae imprisoned by her father to protect her from sex. I painted Persephone in Hades, Eurydice in the land of death, and Eresh-kigal tormented and crucified in the Underworld. I painted the goddess Kore, returning from the Underground to her grieving mother, Demeter. When my mother had read that ancient myth to me, she had said, "See, you're Kore, and, like her, you will always return to your mother."

If any image among the many I was sending up River Road would grab my mother's attention, it would be that one. I strained my mind to reach down river and into my mother's head. Each of the mind-paintings I created, I folded into mental paper airplanes and sent down the road to Mama's house. I had painted my face on my underground heroines before I sailed them, one by one, down river to my mama. She would think of posting them on her refrigerator until it occurred to her what the ESP pictures meant. Then I labored to make the phone ring, until a headache pushed through from the back of my neck to my forehead. When she called and I failed to answer the phone, she would speed down the dusty road between our homes to poke her nose in my business.

Still, silence from above. I did not hear the sound of her Plymouth scratching down the gravel road towards me. I did not feel the wind of her speed on my face. My mother did not come.

When Mildred Dohr's ESP remained unmoved by my artistic renderings, I complained to the waiting walls, "She never did appreciate my art work."

I noticed, though, that I had accomplished something during my unsuccessful attempt at ESP. Having perfected the portrait of me as a classic maiden trapped underground, I remembered I had in mind the mental prototype of a series of paintings I could show at the gallery in September--if ever I could get back upstairs to my sunroom studio. I blew the paint dry on the compassionate maiden Kory, which I had mind-painted in the manner of Rossetti's graceful giantess emerging like the Blessed Damozel above Mt. Hood at dawn. She dove over the berry fields that stretched between the Silky and Mt. Hood, swimming over the world on waves of new sunlight.

I folded that painting into another mental airplane and aimed it out the window grate down River Road towards my mother's house--just in case my ESP experiment might work after all. By this time, she and my father were surely packing their car for their beach trip. I see one of my paper airplanes catch in her hair as she tucks her cosmetics case into the trunk of the car. Thinking it is a wasp or a bird, she brushes it away, but it lands on her clam bucket just as Daddy is about to shut it into the trunk of the car. She sees it is a paper airplane, tells my father to wait a moment before he closes the trunk. She picks up my fragile rice paper airplane and, looks this way and that to see whether Bertie or my father has thrown it. She opens it and sees me, imprisoned. She peers down River Road in my direction. Strains to understand. Gasps and lifts her hand to her mouth.

She gets it!

Mama will come to the back door as always. Knock until the screen door hinges come loose. Look in all the windows. Not see me. Maybe she will have Daddy drive up the dirt road to the quarry at the top of the property to see if I am picking blackberries. Or, she might make him poke around in the meadow above the apple trees thinking I went there looking for inspiration and fell asleep under the boughs at the edge of the orchard.

I could see my mother doing all these things. I imagined my father poking around in the orchard at her bidding, while she came around the south yard, then the front yard and walked down the narrow cement walk right towards the cellar vent. In a moment I would see her ankles through the grid. The tiny perfect dome of a colorless mole on her left shin would gleam like Mt. Hood in the light of day.

Click, click!

Was that the flicker again? He was flick, flick, flicking his beak against the drain pipe. I covered my ears. Flick! Flick! Stuffed wads of newspaper in them. Flick! Then silence. Wait! Had it been the flicker pecking the aluminum down-spout or something else making the noise? Something hard and small against metal. Mama's car key against the window grill?

I pressed my face into the wire window, almost expecting to see my mother's canvas loafers appear six inches from my nose. I slumped back onto my heels and rubbed my knees. I had been so excited, I had knelt beside the vent window and had irritated the scratches on my legs. Overwhelmed by a rush of feelings associated with a hundred scrapes and scratches on which my mother had daubed Mercurochrome with a glass applicator with the globe on the tip, I cried for loneliness.

"Mama!" I called, against all logic. "I'm down here!"

The mama I thought I knew so well should be outside the cellar vent right now, her face pressed up against the wire mesh, calling my name. I felt certain that clicking noise was my mother. She must have driven over to do something Daddy had forgotten to do, perhaps to pick up a toy Bertie claimed he needed to take with him on vacation. My son's face came so clearly to mind, it was almost a palpable presence before me. The strongest feeling that he was nearby infused my being like a full-body blush.

I scrambled across the floor to the cellar door. Peering out the crack between door and frame, I eagerly searched the slice of backyard and driveway I could see for sign of Bertie. Had my son been here? I felt he had. Does a mother's intuition count for nothing? I pressed at the cellar door, as if it must give way for mother love. The door was not sentimental and held firm. There was no car in the drive. But there was something.

Larry's tool chest sat on the sidewalk right at the top of the cellar stairs. Was he here?

"Larry!" I called, banging on the door.

No answer, and no sign of his pickup truck.

I stared at the toolbox as if a pack of circus clowns would tumble out of it and rush down the cellar steps to free me.

How many clowns does it take to open a cellar door?

I don't know, but it only takes one to close one, and his name is Larry.

Laughing bitterly, I slumped against the wall of the stairwell and, in an attempt to understand the presence of the toolbox, I constructed a miniature logic ladder in my mind:

1)   The tool chest was not here before I fell asleep.

2) The tool chest was here after I awoke.

3)   My father's pick-up had been here while I slept.

4) Therefore--Ah, now, I remembered.   Larry's voice reminded me.

Your father asked to borrow my tools.   He promised to bring them back before they left for the beach. Make sure he puts them on the back porch!

Daddy had borrowed Larry's tools.   He had been here, and I had missed him just as I had suspected. But, why had he left the tools on the sidewalk instead of putting them away down cellar the way he used to do his own?

You are so thick, Daddy!

I grabbed a quart jar of peaches by the neck as if it were my father and I was about to throttle him with an as yet undiscovered talent for voodoo. But, when I popped open the inner cap with the can opener provided by my father, I could not stay mad at him. I sighed and, while I ate, began to mull over possible reasons for Daddy's leaving the toolbox on the sidewalk instead of putting it down cellar. Oh. Daddy would have expected Larry to keep his tools down cellar, because that is where Daddy always kept his tools when he lived here.

I sat on my home base on the workbench in the corner by the vent. I drew my knees up to my chin. Squeezing my arms around them, I brooded on the consequences of my father's carelessness, and ate big slippery peach halves.

"Larry will kill me for letting you leave the tools outside to rust," I complained to the air where my daddy once had stood at his workbench. "I don't suppose a metal tool chest will protect metal tools from rust in

Oregon weather, Daddy. If you had the sense to bring a toolbox out of the rain and into the cellar, you might have saved your daughter a world of discomfort."

I thought you were free as a bird and would come across the toolbox and put it away, daughter.

"What if it had rained before I stumbled across the tools?"

"There hasn't been a drop of rain all August, daughter."

"I saw the sun reflected off of clouds when I discovered the closed hasp. And, this is Oregon, remember? We take our clouds seriously."

It isn't raining now, is it? I'm sure the weather will hold until someone can take the tools inside.

"It will be nine days before Larry returns, Daddy."

Seven, not counting today.

"Oh, that's much better. Why didn't you knock on the door and tell me where you had put them, Daddy? Or, if I didn't answer the door, why not put them down cellar? Why leave them out where any passing robber could snatch them?"

"No one passes here, not even robbers. It's a dead end," said my mind-picture of Daddy.

"Tell her the truth, you old geezer," said my mother, adding her bit to my remembered script. "Doc Sully told you you're too old to be lifting anything heavy anymore. Did your father tell you he couldn't even lift the cellar door open, Kory? His toolbox rusted shut because he left it outside. That's why he had to borrow Larry's tools to replace our bathroom doorknob."

"Don't believe your mother, Kory. I told the doc I could lift him and his nurse and throw them both out the window if I wanted."

"Why would I believe my mother's claims?" I said aloud. "I just put my whole self into painting a picture and sending it to her ESP Special Delivery and still she didn't call."

"And that cellar door nearly did you in the last time," Mama said to Daddy, ignoring me. "You couldn't open it at all. I found you collapsed across it with your tongue hanging out. I called the firemen, but, on the way here, they had to extinguish a smoldering stump where some boys had been playing with matches. You nearly expired waiting for them. If you'll remember, that's when we decided to move closer to town."

I had forgotten that, but now I remembered telling Larry about the incident.

If Daddy couldn't open this door, Larry, how did you think I could?

Hidden Hand

Having chug-a-lugged a pint of peaches, I turned my mind to my husband again. He had not realized my plight in a timely and romantic manner--obviously–but might he still put two and two together before I was in real trouble? Without my bidding, a string of imagined scenarios starring Larry swept through my head. In each episode, he would stop suddenly during his fishing trip and realize I was stuck in the cellar. As if I could use sympathetic magic to make him suddenly recall where he had left me --or care about it--I ran the variations of the scenario over and over like a favorite home movie in my head:

Larry flips open his camp stove and puts some canned stew on to heat. While it is warming, he stows the rest of his food in the bear-proof locker, readies his fishing gear for an early start in the morning, and REMEMBERS HE LEFT HIS WIFE LOCKED IN THE CELLAR!

Or, he decides to do some last-minute sunset casting, grabs his pole and tackle box, and strides to the shore of the lake. He sets down his tackle box, sticks a fish egg on the hook, casts off from atop a fallen tree, and is savoring the feel of the sun on his face, the anticipation of the jerk of a fish on his line, and the taste of trout after he has gutted it and fried it in milk, flour, egg and cracker crumbs. But, instead of catching a fish, he catches sight of a line of dark grey smoke rising through the trees. He remembers he has left a little coffee in the pot on the camp stove, and, while he is in a remembering mood, he REMEMBERS HE LEFT HIS WIFE LOCKED IN THE CELLAR!

This fantasy in all its many variations fixed itself in my consciousness, and for hours it would not leave. Eventually, however, even my increasingly speculative mental processes had to give way to practical matters: food, raiment and personal well-being. As to the primal fear of starvation I had been harboring, I figured my treasured can opener had eliminated that cause for alarm.

And, though being shut in small dark spaces gave me the willies, I was probably not going to go mad and attempt to claw through dirt walls to get out of this small dark space. Probably not. Of course, my hope for the productive painting interlude I had been planning for a year had been removed by force from my personal agenda. That disappointment was going to put a crimp in my psyche for a while, but at least I was alive, well fed with regard to at least one of the essential food groups, and--though I was a bit gouged and scraped in spots--relatively well.

I relaxed a bit and surveyed my luncheon possibilities. By the time I had made my choice and guzzled a pint of wild blackberries, the sun had passed overhead. Any fool would have realized by then that the lead-footed driver, Larry, had arrived at the lake yesterday after a long afternoon's drive, and had already had time to do all the things I had imagined would bring him to the realization that I was stuck in the cellar. Even if he had fried a freshly caught trout and was eating it at that very moment by the campfire, he was there and I was here. A hero would have to possess a very long arm to rescue his damsel from such a distance.

Even if Larry should remember right now that he locked me in the cellar, what will he do now that he is too far from home to rescue me? I chose to believe Larry would do what he always did when he needed a hand. He would call his father.

Does your father like me enough to rescue me from a dungeon, Larry?

He didn't like you much after our last card game, Kory.

That canasta game was just one of those awkward occasions, I mused, when people who have known one another for years find out a little more about one another than is good for them to know. There would be an adjustment period, sure, but in another couple weeks, we would all be laughing around Larry's folks' dining-room table about that dreadful card game. And, we would laugh about this ridiculous adventure of mine in the basement too.

If I am even up to playing canasta in a week or two.

But would the supremely competent Lawrence Stamp, Sr., doubt the veracity of a call, even from his son, saying that I, a reasonably intelligent woman, had allowed herself to be buried alive--even if only by accident and if only for a day or so? I asked myself the same question maybe six-hundred times while I was underground. Really, what kind of person could have remained so ignorant of so many things for so long? What other twenty-nine-year-old American had not known of the internment of the Japanese-Americans in World War II, for instance? Larry had known about it while it was happening. As for me, I had not a clue until Larry and his family let the cat out of the bag more than two decades after the fact.

We were playing canasta in the sun room at Larry's folks' house down river from Salmon Run. Seen out the sun room windows, the Silky was living up to its name that August evening, reflecting the moon without a shimmer of distortion. I was deciding whether or not to meld a canasta bit by bit, or to let Larry meld first, or to meld a hidden hand with a flourish, when Larry mentioned to his parents that Nick Nakamura had discussed leasing our bottom land from us.

"Nervy," was Larry's dad's, comment.

"Why nervy?" I asked, double-checking my concealed hand of seven sevens.

Silence dropped over the card table like a tarp.

"Nicky was always courageous on the football field, as I recall, but I'd hardly call him nervy," I persisted.

I kept up the inquisition so long that Larry's mother, Ruth, finally explained with tight lips that the

Nakamura's had harassed the Stamps with "some legal business" once upon a time.

"What sort of legal business?" I asked.

"Really, Kory, it's all over now and we don't like to talk about it," Ruth said.

"Larry and I would like to rent land to Nick, and, if there's bad blood between the two families, wouldn't it be better to clear things up before we enter into an agreement?"

"*I* haven't agreed to enter into it yet," Larry said.

"But you suggested it," I reminded him. "And, why wouldn't you want to enter into the agreement? Nick's always been a good friend."

"To you."

"I thought he was to you too. Whenever we run into him, you two talk about fishing and football until I want to scream. And, forgive me for pointing out the obvious, but weren't the two of you roommates as undergrads?"

"A matter of convenience. We came from the same high school, were in the same math and science classes. Even dated the same girl, as I recall."

"You never dated Donna Yamaguchi!" Ruth exclaimed to Larry.

"I dated Nick once," I shrugged, preparing to meld my canasta of sevens. "When Larry and I were on the outs."

"Your wife dated a Nakamura?" Lawrence questioned his son, folding his cards and covering them with his hand.

"Well, it *was* before we married," I laughed. "But, yes, I asked him to the Sadie Hawkins dance. Larry was mad at me, Donna was out of the picture for some reason, and Nicky had always been sort of like a brother to me."

"Sort of like a brother isn't like a brother at all," Larry muttered, peeking at his cards, which were plastered to his chest.

"You asked *him* out?" Ruth said.

116

"Sadie Hawkins?" I reminded her. "It was a girl-ask-boy dance. I was hoping I wouldn't be broken up with Larry for long and I wanted someone safe to go out with–not someone who would challenge Larry for my hand or something like that."

"If you were thinking so much about me at the time, I wonder why you went out with anyone else at all." Larry snapped.

"You were dating my best friend, Teresa, at the time," I reminded him. "Heavens, I had to do something to take my mind off my grief."

Larry did not appreciate my melodramatic version of events.

"Yeah, that was abject sorrow I saw on your face when you and Nicky were dancing."

"You didn't see me sobbing my eyes out in bed later that night." I leaned across the table and mock-confided to Ruth, "Daddy couldn't sleep due to my sobbing. He told Mama if I couldn't get over Larry, she'd better take me to a psychologist."

"A psychologist, dear?" Ruth asked. The way she said it sounded like, "Axe-murderer, dear?" She was obviously alarmed for the inherited mental health of my offspring, her grandson.

"I didn't go!" I reassured her, laughing. "Your son saved me from that by asking me to go steady with him again."

"I couldn't have Nick Nakamura challenging me for your hand," Larry joked. There was a bitter tang in his voice.

"Oh, yeah, like Nicky would even go steady with me," I chuckled.

"Then I reconciled with you for nothing," Larry joked, picking a card from the top of the deck.

"Wait a minute," I remembered. "How did we get off the subject of the legal battle between the Nakamuras and the Stamps?

"It was nothing," Ruth assured me, giving her discard a dainty thump with her fist.

"I can't imagine the Nakamuras going to law over nothing. They've always been too busy farming around here from dawn to dusk." I drew, and tossed my discard onto the pile.

"They weren't always here farming," Larry disagreed, smugly picking up my discard and tucking it into his hand.

"Always. Except maybe when Nick was out of school sometime between primary grades and high school," I said, rearranging the cards in my hand as if I did not have a canasta. "I don't know where the Nakamuras were then." I looked a question at my father-in-law. He shrugged as he drew, and then discarded. "I have always wondered," I continued, "but Nick wouldn't tell me."

"You are so thick," Larry snorted, arranging the cards in his hand.

"Why?" I asked, drawing a card and discarding it without looking at it. Ruth snatched it up.

"I don't know," he said, "genetics?"

"Why do you say that?" I asked. The conversation was getting so weird.

"Your family ignored the whole thing," Ruth sighed, discarding, "and rightly so."

"What whole thing?" I put my cards face-down on the card table.

"The internment," Larry sighed at my obtuseness. His father grunted his disapproval at the topic of conversation, and his mother bestowed a tight smile upon the proceedings.

"A burial?" I asked. "Whose? A Stamp or a Nakamura?"

"Not an interment," Larry clucked at me. "*The* internment."

I patted my cards into a neat pile and held them in my left hand, tapping them with my thumb. Everyone else held the fans of their cards up high as if to remind me it was my turn.

"What internment?"

118

"Of the Japanese," Larry said, throwing his arms up in the air. "Ta da!"

My mind leapt backward and forward over the intervening years between World War II and that game of canasta with my in-laws. Internment was something that happened in German concentration camps, not in America.

"Concentration camp? Nicky?" I asked, letting my cards fall. They landed face up.

"Look, she's got another canasta," said Lawrence.

"Not again!" said Ruth.

"She always gets canastas," said Larry. His shrill falsetto held the judgment of a gavel's bang.

"But why?" I wondered. "The Nakamura family is more working-for-the-American-Dream than mine is—or than the Stamps."

"The Stamps don't have relatives in their homeland who might persuade them to spy on us," said Lawrence.

"And we were at war with them, dear," Ruth added, counting up my canasta cards with a fingertip.

"We weren't at war with the Nakamuras," I said.

"In a manner of speaking we were," Lawrence snapped, flicking his fanned-out cards with the backs of his fingers.

"In what manner would that be?" I inquired. I really did not like to challenge the elder Stamps, but, for all I knew, the U.S. government had thought the Nakamuras were actually guilty of spying, an idea that I considered as unlikely as any I had ever heard. "In what manner?" I repeated.

"In the manner of physical appearance," Lawrence sighed impatiently.

"I mean, who could tell, really, who was a patriot and who was a spy in those days?" Ruth explained with her kindly air.

"All of us at this table are light-skinned and blondish. Does that mean we should have been jailed as possible German spies during World War II?"

"That wouldn't have been practical, dear," Ruth said, pinching her lips together and studying her cards.

"So, what did they consider practical, putting a few Japanese Americans in a concentration camp to make the public think we were safe?" I asked.

My three card-playing companions concentrated on their hands.

"More than a few?" I croaked.

"All of them," Larry chirped, freezing the deck with a black three.

"Every Japanese American in...?"

"In the West," Larry concluded, "More or less."

"And I didn't know!" A flood of embarrassment at my own ignorance washed me right out of my chair. Brushing my cards off the table onto the floor, I choked and, when I could catch my breath, I ran to the bedroom. I cried for what Nicky had been through--without my being conscious of it for decades. In Larry's old bedroom, where Bertie had been conceived one Christmas vacation, I grieved for my grade school pal, the cute boy who had held my hand on field trips. I grieved for my own ignorance, or blindness—whichever it was. I cried because I was such a complete goose egg. I was not stupid: I had been smart in school. How could I not have known about the internment of Japanese Americans during our childhood? I cried until Larry came to the door and told me it was time to go home.

The next morning, I packed up Bertie and drove to my parents' house. I asked my mother why she had never mentioned that Japanese Americans had been thrown into a concentration camp during World War II-- especially since I had asked her over and over again where Nicky had gone.

Now, in the cellar, remembering interrogating my mother, I wept again. Internment was an issue I mulled over a great deal while I was buried in earth. Something about being imprisoned by a good man–even accidentally–made me think extra hard about why the Japanese Americans had been imprisoned by people I had

thought were good Americans: as a child I had not
sensed that my Japanese American friend had been
interned, and as an adult I had not sensed that a loved one
could imprison me in a cellar. FDR and Eleanor were my
family's primary heroes. How had I missed the clues to
my president's impending disloyalty to his good citizens?
Had I just not listened? Or, had no one even told me?
My mother was a big reader. How had she missed it?
When I asked her that, she echoed the whole German
population, which apparently did not know of the
Holocaust during WWII.

"We did not know." End of subject.

I would have to check at the public library when I
got out of the cellar to find out how much, if anything,
the Oregon newspapers reported about Executive Order
No. 9066 when Roosevelt ordered the internment on
February 19, 1942. Stuck with my own *agayn bite of in
wit*, I had the absurd suspicion that, if I had researched
the internment, I could have sensed that Larry would
subject me to a mini-internment here at home.

You're so thick, Kory, Larry laughed in my head.

After I had interrogated my family about the
matter, I had asked Larry what he knew about how it had
affected the Nakamuras. He told me—as if anyone with
half a brain would know this—that his uncle Gregory
Stamp was the one who was sued by the Nakamuras after
the war when he failed to give them back the farm they
had left in his care while they were interned. I was
stunned to silence until the next morning at coffee when I
got up the nerve to ask my in-laws what came of the
Nakamura-Stamp legal battle.

"We won," Ruth announced with some pride.

"You mean my brother Gregory won," her
husband reminded her.

"Of course."

"What ever happened to the original Nakamura
farm?" I asked Lawrence.

"The law declared it to be the Gregory Stamp farm from the time the Nakamura's sold it to him for a dollar."

"What happened to the farm after your brother died?"

"It became the Stamp farm," he shrugged.

"You hold the deed now?"

"If you want to put it that way."

"Even if Gregory Stamp had told the Nakamuras they could buy the farm back for the same sum when the internment was done?"

"Greg had invested thousands in that land during the war. He transformed it. It wasn't really even the same farm anymore."

"But, in all fairness, it still belongs to the Nakamuras."

"The law doesn't see it that way."

"But, morally...."

"I'm not giving it back," Grampa Lawrence grinned in that mischievous one-sided way he had. "Besides, they have their own farm now."

"That was their own farm."

"Lots of those people lost their farms. Everybody was doing it. They have a new farm now. What more could they want?"

"Justice?"

"The whole thing is water under the bridge!" Lawrence, Sr., puffed. "It's too late to do anything about it."

"You could sign over the deed to the surviving sons, Nicky and his brother."

"Since Greg died, it has been mine. The rents off that land put your husband through college. Why would I sign it over to the Nakamuras?"

"Because it would be right?"

"Right is a relative term–relative to whose relatives you want to support, your own or somebody else's," he chuckled.

"Well, I could rent the plot Nicky wants to farm for a dollar a year is what I could do relative to somebody else's relatives," I said. I snapped off a piece of shortbread and popped it into my mouth.

"Better see what your husband has to say about renting to the Nackamuras," Big Lawrence said.

"My folks deeded it to--" I stuffed another piece of shortbread into my mouth to prevent myself from reminded the Stamps that I alone owned the property.

Grampa Lawrence held his lips tight and stirred his coffee.

"It may be your land, but you're his wife," Ruth reminded me.

The muffling family tarp fell down over the table again until Larry broke the silence.

"We'll just see about renting land to Nick Nackamura," Larry sneered, pretending to twirl his villain's mustache.

"I only want what's fair," I said, taking another sip of coffee.

Coffee was sipped, eyes squinted, resentments surfaced. I stirred a drop of artificial sweetener into my cup.

"Who told you the world was fair?" Lawrence grinned, leaning back in his chair and pulling his belt down below his belly.

"All it takes is one fair hand to begin to shape a fair world," I said.

"Who said that?" Ruth asked, to change the subject.

"No one did. Kory makes up quotations to give weight to her many opinions," Larry said, rolling his eyes with meaning at his dad.

"It's true," I shrugged. "I make up quotations. I eat too much shortbread. I lose at cards on purpose sometimes. Obviously, there's something wrong with me. I would like to think I am a fair person though, no matter what the rest of the world may think."

"In a small town, I'm afraid it matters what the world thinks," said Ruth.

"In a family it matters what people think," Lawrence snorted.

Quickly Larry gave me the married people's head beckon, thanked his folks for the coffee, and woke Bertie from a nap. I gathered up Bertie's things, and we three went home.

On the five-mile drive down River Road to our house, I studied Larry across the front seat. Bertie was babbling loudly about a "bigga bug" he had seen on his Gramma Ruth's rose bushes that day. *Hadda funny tail and a speak like a bird an' wings bigga than the whole rests of him. What was it, Mommy, that bigga bug?*

Before I could answer, Larry--without turning his face from the road–said, "The supporting architecture of a family can be weakened, my pretty little termite, and ultimately destroyed by one disloyal nibble."

Lying in my quiet cellar after recalling that grim little family scene, I recalled that one of the last things Larry had said before he slammed the cellar door in my face was: *Some threats to mutual loyalty can destroy a family forever.* Did that mean his parents would cut me off forever, because I questioned their dealings with the Nakamuras? Until the friction between us a few nights ago, I had never thought of Larry's family as having any strong feelings about anything except having the right to bear arms and having the right scotch on hand for happy hour every evening. But, now that I had stuck my foot in my mouth all the way to my duodenum, would Larry's father refuse to free me from my prison, even if Larry wanted me to be freed? I tried to concentrate on the hope that my father-in-law would come to save me despite my short sightedness and pesky lust for justice. Humans are as capable of finding extreme remedies to disasters as they are to creating difficulties for one another, I hoped.

When Nicky disappeared during World War II, why didn't I ask everyone I met where he had gone, until I found somebody who would tell me?

The question lay heavy and turgid on my brain, but I had more immediate problems. I was hungry again, for one thing. For another, I had to pee. With my lovely can opener, I opened a pint jar of rhubarb pie filling and half-ate, half-drank its contents, then carried the jar step by newspaper-protected step across the dirt floor and refilled it with what I had had for lunch. Then I replaced the rubber-rimmed cap and the ring, cleaned my hands as well as I could and fell over on the work bench, exhausted from trying to figure out if anybody on earth considered me worth saving.

Nicky, I thought, and a wave of shame burned me in my chilly underground dwelling. How in the world had he ever forgiven me?

The Way the Earth Smells

Nicky Nackamura, seven years old with a mischievous glint in his eye, had accepted a challenge to braid my hair after his cousin Bradley teased me in the schoolyard.

"Your hair look like you sticking you finger in a light socket," is what Bradley had said. As I was hanging upside down on the chinning bar at the time, I took that as an unfair comment. Skinning the cat, I landed right at his feet and asked him how he liked my hairdo close up.

Bradley said, "Maybe if you comb it once awhile."

I could see by my shadow in the schoolyard dirt that my hair was sticking up like light bulb filaments, and I argued some more about how much easier life was for boys and their short hair and how hard braiding was for girls.

"How hard could that be?" Bradley laughed.

"How would I know?" I fumed, "My mother braids my hair."

Bradley scoffed, "I braided a plastic key chain in kindergarten."

"Does my hair look plastic?"

"It look spastic," Bradley snickered.

Nick took my hand, led me to the swings, sat me down on one and unbraided my hair. Bradley stood there gaping at us. A tittering primary school crowd gathered, while Nick ran his fingers through my hair, blew the strays off my face and neck and braided my wispy tresses in one braid down my back. I tried to keep a straight face, but I know my eyes were laughing with triumph over Bradley. Reason might say that Nick had proved his cousin's point that anyone can braid, but I had Nicky's soft hands in my hair. His breath smelled like Almond Roca.

In my cellar, I pulled my apron up over my neck. The tantalizing aroma of Almond Roca seemed to fill my dirt cell. It smelled like rescue. Whether or not he had intended to, Nick had come to save me that day in the schoolyard, but now I had run out of reasons any family members might come rescue me. And, by virtue of his character and despite my ignorant response to the great tragedy of his early life, Nick seemed a more likely candidate to be a hero than any of the rest of them.

Nicky and I had been best friends in school, holding hands on the way to recess, to assembly, to gym class, to the restrooms. The practice continued until school policy dictated that we were old enough to be trusted not to separate from our classmates and go running in front of passing cars. I, for one, regretted the discontinuation of the hand-holding protocol, because Nicky's hand was so welcoming, and softer than satin. Plus, he taught me a game he called hand tag, in which one of his fingers would dart in and out among mine and I would have to catch his with one of my fingers. We could play that game all the way from the classroom to the school bus without the teacher catching on. Nicky always won, but I did not mind much.

What impressed me more than Nicky's playfulness was that, while we were hand-holding partners, he never once let go of my hand. When I was a toddler, my mother had kept me in tow with a dog leash. Later, she kept me next to her by willpower--never by holding hands. I also remembered that there were callouses on Nicky's palms from his hanging from tree limbs and the monkey bars, but, even so, holding his hand was like holding marshmallow candy. I fell in love with his hand before I fell for his impish black eyes or later with the smooth tan calves that showed below his football knickers, or his eloquent, compact back. Once we got to the school yard, he would let go my hand and run off to play with his rough friends, but once in a while we would end up hanging side by side on the monkey bars. Our upside down conversations always fascinated me.

"Do you like the way the earth smells?" he once asked me.

"You mean, like dirt?"

"Like this dirt. Here, smell it."

"Eeuuu, Nicky! Smells dirty."

"To me, it smells like all the wonderful things that could grow in it."

The small wounds I had suffered in the cellar would wake me from time to time. Every time my fingertips or knees began to tingle and then to sting, inconsiderate things I had said to Nick before I found out about the internment would nettle my conscience. Though I was interred in a place not designed for human comfort, how much worse must Nick's internment have been?

Ooo, Kory, you are so sensitive. That was Larry in my head, helping me along with my regrets as usual. *That itty bitty bee sting isn't exactly the Bataan Death March, sweetie.* No one could argue with that.

One day, before Nick disappeared from school, we had one of our conversations on the monkey bars. I was wearing a cotton pinafore and felt the spring breezes warming my bare thighs. Nicky was hanging upside down beside me in a clean white tee shirt and jeans with fine-patched knees.

"Look, I'm coming un-rooted!"

"What's that mean?" I called to him. "Don't you mean uprooted?"

"I dunno," Nicky called back. "I feel funny in the feet."

I had no idea what that meant, but it made us laugh.

Soon after that, a quirky spring storm iced up the roads and we had a few days off from school. I do not think it was a silver thaw, but it felt like one. It was cold. Nicky and I were seven. With the schools closed, all the children were at home in our neighborhood when the bottom fell out of America. For years afterwards I dangled alone in air with no support under me and never even noticed. When the rest of us returned to school after the ice storm, Nicky and his cousin Bradley had disappeared from the school roster. They did not return to Salmon Run until after the war.

On my ersatz bed in the cellar, I gingerly caressed my scratched fingers while shame burned my face. *At least my face is warm.* Recalling my very tardy awareness of the internment made me feel sick. Remembering Larry's words enhanced the effect.

Wasn't the internment something too huge to miss?

No matter how I tore at my memory, I could not recall hearing of the internment in all those years. Even at Sacagawea Union High School, where history was my favorite subject after art, we never heard tell of the internment. Probably not an officially sanctioned school subject in a district heavily populated with Japanese-American farmers. And, in the twenty years between the evacuation and my tardy cognizance of it, my parents had not once mentioned at the dinner table that American citizens had been imprisoned in concentration camps. You would think that even my non-political parents would have discussed it in passing--especially when I went around the house moaning, "Where'd Nicky go, anyway?" Nicky's family's loss of their farm was not the sort of news item that the *Salmon Runner* would report, but my folks subscribed to the *Riverport Review*, and, several national magazines as well. How could we have missed news which affected our neighbors so drastically?

I concluded that even I must have heard news of the internment of Japanese Americans from some source. To assuage my guilt feelings, I made a mental list of possible excuses for my having overlooked the cause of Nicky's disappearance. For one thing, I would never have suspected Uncle Sam of such a betrayal of his citizens. His picture was everywhere. I knew him better than I knew God or Jesus. And, even though Uncle Sam pierced me with his stern look whenever I ran into one of his *Uncle Sam Wants YOU* posters, I trusted him and–if not for the Ten Commandments or my inconvenient empathy--would have gone to war myself if he had asked. Since I could not have imagined Uncle Sam's signing Executive Order 9066, how could I have guessed that my family's hero, President Franklin Delano Roosevelt, had ordered the Secretary of War to separate Japanese Americans from the general population? I was not a regular reader of the newspaper at the age of seven, but I brought it in from our paper box on the street every day. Maybe I glimpsed word of the event, but did not know what evacuated meant. Or perhaps the news had been slipped into the paper in the tiny print reserved for huge matters thought best left unheralded. I blushed to recognize that one of my shortcomings has always been a failure to take an interest in the fine print. And, maybe– though I cringed to think it–the news was delivered in big, fat print, but to my parents–immersed like the majority of the populace in the pervasive context of war-- it had seemed just another nasty bit of news, not remarkably different from any other tidbits of gossip about humans mistreating humans.

It was not as if second and third graders of my acquaintance ignored the national news. The hot news among citizens my age was that the Japanese attack on the west coast of America was imminent. The first planes had probably already flown over my house. Regularly, among primary schoolers, the news went round that the end of the world would happen within the week. In fact, I recall seeing only one headline during World War II: **THE END OF THE WORLD TOMORROW.** I admit I did not take it as the gospel when my school friends showed it to me, but I did keep an extra-sharp eye out for enemy planes in the sky for some time after that.

Partly because of my age during the war, and also, I suspect, because I have always been visually oriented, I took in the news chiefly through pictures. And, I had always been fascinated and horrified by stories and pictures about children distressed by war. Every week, I had studied the photographs in *Life,* and I had pored over the pictures in our copy of their pictorial volume on World War I. Now, I riffled through them by the hour in my dirt-walled mental movie theater, but I found no photos of the internment. Had the subject been at least pictured in *Life?* The only picture in my life I failed to study hard enough was the one with Nicky suddenly not in it. *Un-rooted.* Now, in the intimacy of my dirt dwelling, my failure to read between the lines loomed large, leaving me feeling I was an accomplice in both my internment and Nicky's.

At the time he disappeared, I thought Nicky's funny-feeling feet had been a sign of some horrible disease of the extremities and that his family had moved somewhere that had a good foot hospital. But, why when Nick reappeared, had I not even asked where he had been? Years after his disappearance, I saw Nicky in the hallway at school. It was our first day as freshmen at Sacagawea High. Though he was two feet taller than last time I saw him, I would have recognized him in a blinding snow storm. I felt shy and a bit resentful. Even then I had not heard where Japanese Americans from the west coast had spent the war. For so many ignorant years, I had the impression that Nicky had left me specifically and on purpose and not because our trusted Uncle Sam had slapped him and his family into a concentration camp.

"How are your feet?" is what I offered to Nicky as my first greeting in years.

"They keep my ankles from scraping the ground," he smiled quizzically.

"And your hands, were they affected too? They must be healed by now or they wouldn't let you into high school."

"Healed?" Nicky frowned. "I could still beat you at hand tag," he smiled.

He stubbornly refused to see that I was trying to get him to tell me where he had been for almost a decade.

"You had no access to pen and paper," I sniffed, "so you couldn't write a letter, a note, a scrap of a message in a bottle?"

"Oh," Nicky nodded, getting it. "No, we didn't have. Not for a long time."

"What's that supposed to mean? You never even said goodbye, but couldn't you have written it?"

"No, I could not."

"They didn't have pens and paper where you went?"

"Not much."

"Pens and paper practically grow on trees in the civilized world," I protested.

"Yes, in the civilized world," he said. "But, even if I had had the means...," he mumbled, "Shame is ... a powerful deterrent."

"Shame?" I demanded, loudly enough to cause half the freshmen in the school corridor to stop poking around in their lockers and stare at us.

"Why? Were you in jail?" I laughed.

He blushed and turned away from me. I was mystified by his embarrassed tone.

"What have you got to be ashamed of?" I was beginning to think maybe he had spent the intervening years between the primary grades and high school in jail.

"I've got nothing to be ashamed of," he flared. His face turned a deep maroon, leaving only a golden islet, his perfect nose tip. "But when the persecutor feels no shame, the victim feels it for him."

He slammed his locker shut, and, hoisting his books up under his arm pit, he made his way through the crush of freshmen in the hall. I stood dazed for a moment. I had never seen Nicky angry like that. I ran after him.

"I'm sorry," I puffed, when I finally caught up to him outside Algebra I. "Have I persecuted you somehow?"

He wheeled on me and pinned me against some sophomore's locker. I raised my books to keep his notebook from poking me in the breasts. I must have looked terrified and bewildered because Nicky pulled back immediately.

"Not you. You were always a friend." He tweaked my cheek hard with his marshmallow-candy hand and strode off down the hallway. By the time my mind had emerged from the shadows, I could not have followed him if I had wanted to. He met Donna Yoshida half way to the stairwell, and, throwing his arm around her shoulder, he entered the World History classroom where they would learn a version of events that would leave out the momentous part played by Japanese Americans during World War II.

Still smells like Almond Roca.

By the time we were sophomores in high school, I had forgiven him for disappearing without a word. I did not confront the reason for his absence, though, until I managed to get trapped in my own cellar.

After high school, I lost touch with Nick and Donna while we attended rival Oregon universities. During those years, the Nakamura clan members worked their way up from field workers to farm owners again. Nicky and Donna married and were living on the new Nakamura farm next to his father's former farm on the bluff above my parents' land, and I married Larry and went to grad school back east. While there, I painted images of the farm country in the Mt. Hood watershed, still without knowing certain truths about the area of my birth that would one day embarrass me.

For a moment, I stopped caressing my sore fingers and called Nick's name aloud to the empty cellar, as if I could draw him to me. My voice had returned after resting for some hours, and I gave a brief joyful laugh at hearing it again. In the process, I dropped my apron off the workbench. Tears started in my eyes, but, lying on my belly on the bench, I managed to catch one corner of the apron and pull it up onto my body.

I've no right to call out to my past to come save me in the present. Besides, I'd die of embarrassment if the hero of Sacagawea High School's football team found me here with my neat row of used canning jar chamber pots lined up against the dirt wall. But if Nick were my only hope to get out of the cellar? He had been awfully insistent about leasing that land down by the river. And he was under a time constraint. Maybe he would come back to taste our dirt again. Maybe he would drop by to see me as he had promised he would do once he got the lease. *And maybe a rogue tornado will come by and lift the house off this cellar so I can walk up the steps to freedom.*

I sighed, recalling that I had as good as put up a No Trespassing sign until after Larry got back. Not likely Nick would be dropping by until then.

Folding myself into a tiny ball and ruminating on my chances of being rescued always ended the same way: in disbelief and depression. Whenever I engaged in actual work towards improving my lot in the cellar, though, my optimism and my fantasy of being rescued would be reborn. I smoothed out my apron while I worked up a scenario of Nick rescuing me momentarily. *Isn't it true that he is still attracted to me? Maybe not the way he was attracted to his cheer leader girlfriends, but in some special way? He as good as asked me to paint his portrait. What better time than when Larry's gone? Of course! That would be the only time I could paint Nick. He must know that!*

After I had smoothed out my apron, which had become tangled from my twisting and turning on my wooden bed, I crawled under it and smoothed it over me as best I could. I blushed to concede that Larry was right about one thing: Nick and I did share a look now and then which told of long mutual knowledge. I smiled at the thought that Nick might be drawn by some magical sympathy to visit me soon. As I squirmed under my apron, it fell to the floor again. *Bad sign.*

I climbed down to fetch it, reflecting that, though Nick had never reciprocated my invitation to the Sadie Hawkins dance, he had not had a chance. Larry had asked me to go steady again the very next day after that dance. Then I recalled another example of Nick's and Larry's competition. Larry had cut in on us on the floor at the Sadie Hawkins Dance, and Larry and his date (my best friend Teresa) even turned up at Hung Far Lo, the Chinese restaurant where Nick took me after the dance. Larry got all jolly and suggested we share a table at the restaurant. Now that I thought about it, Larry had played "kneesies" with me under the table. If Nick had not paid the bill and whisked me out of the restaurant while Larry and Teresa were in the restrooms, they might have followed us up to Devil's Elbow. With a thrill, I realized Nick had tried to get me away from Larry, at least that one time. *There was evidently more than one event I was dense about when I was a girl.*

Momentarily, I was warmed by my imaginative reasoning. *Nick will come for me!* I duck-walked the length of the workbench to fetch a quart of pears from the fruit shelf. *But, maybe not today.*

To lift my spirits, which had been yo-yoing with alarming speed, I opened the pears and toasted myself with the juice before gulping it down. The ragged shreds that had sloughed off of the pears clung to the surfaces of the liquid and I had to force myself not to gag. Spoiled on the purest water in the world provided by the Mt. Hood watershed, I had never had to endure things floating in my beverage. As always, however, my sparse meal exhilarated me for a moment.

As soon as I had finished wiping my chin with a dainty scrap of *The Salmon Runner*, I lay down on my wooden bed and rolled onto my side while splinters the size of green beans caught at my flimsy dress. Blocking out the gloom by laying my forearm over my eyes, I felt the construct of hopes regarding Nick begin to crumble around me again. As I pulled my apron up over my shoulder, I wished that I could sink into the workbench boards and disappear. No one was going to come for me. I was filthy. I had chronic fantasies about an old crush. I peed in a jar.

During my stay in the cellar, my mood must have plunged from optimism to despair and back again a thousand times. Once, as I lay there and my body heat began to warm the air spaces trapped under the leatherette apron, I mused that I had survived traumas before: I had lost my best friend to the vortex of suspicion caused by a world war, and I had found out within the past week that my beloved Uncle Sam had a dark side. I had even had to face the fact that my husband might not be as jolly inside as he was outside. So, some of my heroes were not always heroic! Maybe I would prove heroic enough to make up for the lack of damsel-rescuers hereabouts.

Not as heroic as Nicky, though. I thought about what courage it must have taken to achieve high school fame on the football field through his strengths, when he had been treated so badly by his own government. What confidence he and his family must have in their rights as citizens to come back to Salmon Run, where they had been cheated and betrayed by their best friend. I had never been sent away by the government and I had much less confidence in my right to be myself than Nick did.

Too drained to parse that paradox with logic, I thought I could probably only understand it by mind-painting a picture of me and Nicky together as children, before he was taken away. Before one brush stroke could fall in my weary mind, however, night fell, turning the dim light from the vent into the velvet cerement of no light at all. So shrouded, I fell asleep with my cheek against the restless dirt wall. I slept fitfully and dreamed an icky dream: Nicky was calling me. Something so horrible had happened to him and the group of his friends surrounding him that I was afraid to look closely at the little girl holding his hand.

Fortunately, all good nightmares must come to an end. I woke to darkness, feeling hungry, damp, and troubled by the idea that I had collaborated somehow in Nicky's internment. And always, the sound of Larry's laughter ran in rills through the pathways of my mind.

It ain't the Bataan Death March, sweetie.

Silver Thaw

The first few nights I spent in the cellar I had one piece of good luck: The fine August heat wave had not yet given way entirely to the inevitable September chill. Every night I tried to go to sleep and stay asleep from the time night blacked out the vent window until dawn grazed it with a pale curtain of light. Each time I awoke, I would backpedal furiously towards dreamland, dreading the nightmare that would greet me upon waking. Though I might not make it all the way back to sleep, I often managed to hover in a dreamlike memory of my best days aboveground.   Into those recollections, my imaginary wild-Indian playmates came often and stayed long.

I remembered that, after the weather cooled each fall, the Native American family's visits to the cove across the river became less frequent.   Sometimes the water would be warm enough for one more swim before winter, but on cooler days, the braves would poke their toes into the water, and run back to their mother squealing and shivering.   Then she would gather her children around her on her blanket, and, huddled together with them under a lean-to tent made up of two cottonwood branches and a second blanket, she would tell stories to them. The wind would carry many of the words away, but from my hiding place under the blackberry vine, watching her plump hands describing birds in flight, leaping mountain lions, or swimming fish, I understood her stories well enough.

As a white person of European descent living on Native American soil, I always considered myself a squatter. I felt the Native American mother's tales were held in trust in the very soil which my family owned but which I thought of as having been borrowed from the Native Americans. But, because I had grown up on that land, I believed I had ingested elements of Native American myths the way a flower draws nutrients from the soil. Now, half-asleep and imbedded in that soil, I shrank away from the cooling damp walls and, to warm myself, tried to remember those warm days spent watching that family across the river.

The tale I recalled was the one that had informed the painting I had lost called *Silver Thaw*--the one I had originally planned to recreate this week for my gallery showing. As I drifted in and out of sleep, I listened for the voice of the native mother telling the Warm Wind Brothers' tale, and, imagining I lay in my tunnel under the berry vines, at last I heard her:

"Everywhere the Warm Wind Tribe traveled, fair weather prevailed. The tribe thrived, until they were discovered by the Cold Wind Tribe, whose presence would turn the local weather so cold that everything froze and life became impossible. The Warm Wind Tribe moved south again and again, but every time, the Cold Wind Tribe followed and froze the land until it was uninhabitable. After many cycles of this warming and freezing, and challenges between the two tribes–which were always won by the Cold Wind brothers--the Warm Wind Tribe was at a loss as to how to improve their fortunes."

As I remembered the native mother's voice describing the plight of the Warm Wind brothers and envisioned her brown hands showing how birds turned crystalline in the air at the approach of the Cold Wind tribe, how bears froze in their dens and squirrels were struck numb on tree branches, I saw *Silver Thaw* repaint itself before me. In that painting of the first silver thaw I ever experienced, a small figure in red was frozen in flight at the top of the arc of a swing strung from the branch of a leafless cherry tree. All the trees and shrubs wore heavy ice cloaks and the ground hid under a thick blanket of snow and a patina of ice. The sky was a piercing blue on both sides of the river, but only on the near side did it look down on a deep-frozen scene. A flicker was flash-frozen on the wing, the swing was frozen suspended in the air, the small figure in the red snowsuit at the top of the swing's arc was so hypnotized by her flight that she appeared carved from a large ruby.

When Mama had put me into a new red snowsuit the day of my first silver thaw, so eager was I to get outside and play in the snow that I had not cared that I was zipped into it up to my eyebrows. But, Mama did not let me play outdoors that day. I was only allowed to swing for a moment while she snapped my picture in my new snowsuit. When I was at the top of the swing's arc, though, I saw the braves sledding across the river, beyond the blackberry vines. Then Daddy quickly lifted me out of my swing and Mama took one more snap of me licking the ice off broken twigs before pulling me towards the house.
"No, Mama!" I cried, "I want to go sledding with my playmates across the river!"
"We don't play with imaginary children," Mama informed me and dragged me into the house.

Across the river, in my painting, the native children were sledding, but not on snow. Across the Silky, it was summer and they were sledding in dishpans down a sandy bank into the water. I had smiled whenever I looked at the picture I had painted, gazing at the almost invisible Warm Wind warrior's figure entwined in a warm zephyr moving across the Silky River. I had embedded that hero from the native mother's tale of the *Warm Wind* brothers in that painting because he represented the triumph over mutability in nature (or in human nature) symbolized by the silver thaw. I longed to tell Larry the theme of the painting, but he hated to hear such tripe, as he called anything you could not measure with a thermometer, a rain gauge or a wind sock.

As a weatherman, I think, Larry was a bit intrigued with the picture, but he never could understand

140

why a warm breeze had melted the snow and brought out the leaves and blossoms on the trees across the river, when on our side of the Silky everything was covered in thick layers of ice.   Being doggedly science-minded, he could not have been expected to see the native hero traveling by cloud, or to decipher the meaning of a scene split between two seasons. My thinking on the other hand was about as mechanical and routine as a leaf blown about by a rascally wind, and thus I could feel the cold on my side of the river and long for the warmth on the other side.

Despite his intolerance for the picture, Larry took it to a shop to get it matted and framed as a surprise for my birthday.   The proprietor smiled, asking who had *tried to paint the primitive watercolor--Gramma Moses' drug addict granddaughter.* Larry mumbled something inaudible to the man, took back the unframed picture and slunk out of the shop.   He brought the painting back home and, when I returned from grocery shopping, he brought my painting into the kitchen and placed it on the kitchen table.

His face often turned a deep red when he was upset about something, but that time I noticed his ears were red too.   And his neck, all the way round to the back.   He told me then what his lovely plan for my birthday present had been and what the horrible man had said to him.   I felt sorry for the pain Larry must have suffered, but knew immediately I should not let pity show on my face.   He shoved the painting across the table at me, rather roughly, I thought.   At the time I believed the gesture expressed his anger at the tactless art critic.

"I'm sorry," I said.   I meant I was sorry for the way the man had treated him, not for the painting I had painted. The painting was like one of the essential organs of my body.

"Find a hobby you can actually get good at, kiddo," he said.   He looked jolly (though red), but his words snapped at me like nylon fish line on an icy day.

"Is that any way to talk to Gramma Moses?" I murmured, looking away.

"We don't want this painful thing between us," Larry said, softening his voice and reaching for my chin to turn my face towards him. I thought he was going to wrap his arms around me and apologize for taking his pain out on me. "Come on," he commanded, "and bring that with you." With a flip of his hand, he indicated the painting. I slid it off the table and followed him. I thought we were going to take it to another frame shop where we might be treated better. I was about to remind Larry that I had just put Bertie down for his nap, when I saw where Larry was headed.

He went out the back door, across the driveway and stopped before the oil drum where we always burned our trash. It lay on its side with the cold ashes of a cereal box falling out its mouth. The front panel of cardboard had burned but without disintegrating into soot and, I could still read the brand name Cap'n Crunch and see the Cap'n with his blue nautical hat and coat and his spyglass. I thought of how *Silver Thaw* would look burned but still intact, like the same image, only painted on ebony, and so ephemeral that all the work and love I had put into it could be blown away with one breath. I hugged the painting to me.

Larry did not tear it from my grasp. If he had, the pain might not have seared so deep. He took it from me as the midwife takes the tender babe from its mother's breast when it has fallen into blissful sleep after nursing. He threw a match onto a pile of unburnt milk cartons, and, when a fine flame was crackling, he forced *Silver Thaw* in through the mouth of the oil drum. I did not collapse in on myself, fall to my knees and keen and wail, although that is what I wanted to do. The painting may not have been Turner or Rossetti, but it was as precious as a child to me. Maybe things would have been different if I had shown what I felt. But I was frozen like the girl on the swing in the painting. Watching the flames feast on the colors and canvas, I saw only the icy scene I had painted melting away. The fire of Larry's anger was as the ice along our side of the riverbank to me. In one action my husband poured hot and cold running rage on my painting--and on my desire to be an artist by definition and in practice.

Larry lay his arm heavily across my shoulders and guided me into the house.

"I went through your sketches and paintings while you were out shopping," he soothed. "I wadded up the ones that don't pass muster and we will burn them too."

The ice encasing me melted a little in a spurt of anger.

"Art work that wouldn't pass muster with that shop owner?" I asked. I could not believe he would say yes, but he did.

"If he had raped me, would you think my body had not passed muster and burn it in the trash can?"

"On the contrary," he laughed, "I would think he thought your body passed muster too well."

"Larry," I choked, "Did it ever occur to you that the man who criticized my painting was not the spokesman for the entire art world? Did you consider the possibility he might be wrong?"

That is what I said, but all that came out my mouth was, "He might be wrong?"

"He doesn't even know us. Why would he lie?" said my husband.

I experienced an instant case of Novocain tongue and could not reply: My anger had frozen atop layers of melted and re-frozen indignation. *I'm a goddamn silver thaw.* While I was incapable of responding aloud, my husband explained himself, saying, "Sometimes you express yourself too impulsively, Kory, thus leaving yourself open to ridicule. And, leaving me open to it too, I might add."

Most of my life, I had seen Larry and me as a natural pair living amid unchanging, secure families along the Silky. Recalling the fate of my *Silver Thaw*, however, in the light of my recent discovery of Nicky's fate during the war, I questioned the immutability of such things as family and country. Stumbling upon that thought, I remembered I was still in the cellar and that I had opened my eyes on a cold day with no discernable sky. Realizing that anything in nature or society could be altered drastically without warning, I felt the energy to repaint *Silver Thaw* evaporate in the cooling cellar air.

"Although, paper, paints, brushes and familial encouragement might have inspired me," I grumbled. "Or breakfast!"

I roused myself to plan my day as I would have planned any other day alone, starting with the basics, and not even mind-painting until said mind had been nourished. What's for breakfast? (Canned fruit, same as yesterday.)   What shall I wear today? (Threadbare muumuu, same as yesterday.) Any appointments today? (Ha ha.) How well-groomed shall I be? (Crap in a jar, wash yourself as well as you can with newspaper, and comb your hair with your dusty fingers.) Arrange palette, canvas and easel for today's planned painting. (Blackberry juice smeared on a denim bib on the workbench?)

First I scanned the fruit shelf to make my menu selection, undisturbed by the knowledge that I was showing early signs of a monster case of diarrhea. Why, I wondered? Fruit does not usually do that to me. How little I knew then of the forces at work in my viscera. Having set forth my agenda, I fetched my can opener from its nail, and opened a pint of Freestone peaches, (A healthy diet is a varied diet.) After eating several sleek and golden peach halves, I gulped down the sweet gloppy bath in which they had floated. As I drank, I realized the shreds of fruit floating in the liquid did not bother me as they had at first. Was I becoming an aficionado of cellar cuisine? As I went through the motions of cleaning the juices off my hands and face with newspaper, I wondered what other tastes of mine might be changing.   Then, as was my custom, I refilled the jar with the leavings of a pint of pears I had processed overnight, recapped it and stacked it on the pyramid in the far corner with the others I had filled.

While completing my ablutions, a wisp of hope that I could execute, stroke by stroke, (in my mind) my design for *Silver Thaw* began to grow again.

Who will paint it, Gramma Moses on drugs?

My mind was still too full of such discouraging words to allow room for *mind-painting*, I found. Besides, I needed to create something more practical that day. I had noticed that the cellar had not warmed up at all after dawn. It did not take a weatherman to notice that last night the temperature had seemed inclined to plunge over the edge into true cold. I would have to create some means of keeping warm or the coming night would likely be unbearably cold. I decided my art project of the day would be a patchwork quilt.

I had seen the building blocks of my quilt my first day in, but had rejected them as potential tools for my survival. They were so filthy that even the fastidious Larry had not deigned to pluck them out of the greasy bit of cardboard box on which they lay on the top shelf above the canned fruit. My guess was that Daddy had used the oil rags to wipe his hands after he had opened a can of motor oil with the sacred can opener and then tossed them out of sight. I found unsettling the knowledge that such fine fuel for a house fire had lain under Bertie's floor just inches from his bed the whole year he had slept here. Though a coverlet drenched in motor oil was not my idea of an accoutrement of a luxurious boudoir, it was better than the alternatives at hand. I pushed myself to my feet, and, hunching over to avoid bonking my head on the beams, I duck-walked across the workbench to the fruit shelves, reached up and brought down the cardboard box full of oily rags– and, with it, a family of hairless baby mice.

There were two of them and they were smaller and pinker than my little fingers. Their mama was not at home at the moment, and for a horrible second I considered squashing the poor little things. Their eyes were not open yet, so it is not as if they would have seen it coming. They had landed safely atop the workbench, still in the box and still on a soft mattress of oily rags. Their rest disturbed, they were moving around in circles, sniffing the air for scent of their mother, I supposed, rather the way I had been sniffing for sight or sound of my own mother the day before. Fellow orphans. I lifted from the box the rag serving as their nest. The mother had made a comforter of her own downy hair, chewed cardboard (from the underlying box, which was severely tattered), and bits of unidentifiable fabric and plant fluff. Holding the nest in my right hand, I threw the tangled mass of rags on the workbench behind me, and tucked the nest into its protective corner in the box before replacing it on the top shelf. I worried for a moment that the mouse dander on any blanket I fashioned out of the rags would probably draw their mother to my sleeping body. Possibly she would think her babies were tucked into the folds of my quilt and would nose about in there looking for them. I hoped she would be more like my mother and fail to notice her babies were not where they should be.

The rags were of the sort that you see lying around on service station workbenches, gold, blue or rose-colored, cotton, loosely woven, with bound edges rather than hems. They had some sort of blue writing printed on them, but, as it was probably not edible, I did not bother to read it. I focused on figuring out a way to bind the squares together. I tried biting the thread of a hem in order to pull it free of the cloth and sew it to another rag. Even if the cloth had not frayed, making it unfit to lash two pieces together, the smell of mouse would have prevented me from doing that twice. And, by the way, where was the needle with which to bind them?

After spending the morning shaking out the rags in my "privy" corner, and rubbing them vigorously to get as much offal out of them as I could, I spread them out atop my workbench bed and considered how to make the squares stick together as a quilt. I could not help but

146

notice that, without thinking, I had laid the gold and pink pieces out in a pattern very pleasing to behold.

It ain't Picasso, but if I wrapped myself in Guernica, *would it keep me warm?*

I had no needle, but I did have the can opener (Thank you again, Daddy), which I used to poke holes inside the hem all around each oil rag. These holes were large enough to allow a bobby pin to slip through them. Fortunately, there was that one bobby pin in my apron pocket. Who had dropped it and kicked it under the bottom workbench shelf where I had found it on my first day is not known, but it gave me an idea. After opening a jar of applesauce and sucking it down, I closed the jar and set it aside to refill later as needed. Then I climbed onto the workbench at the foot of my unassembled blanket and began plucking hairs out of my head. My mother and mother-in-law had hinted for years that most ladies cut their schoolgirl locks by the time they reached the far end of their twenties. However, my long hair was one of the few elements of the image as a bohemian artist I had retained after housewifery had stripped me down to the essentials of American womanhood. I took a few strands of hair, braided them, threaded them through the "eye" of the bobby pin, and pushed the head of the bobby pin alternately through a hole on one rag and then the one next to it.

Finally got your head out of those watercolor clouds and down to earth, eh, daughter?

I always aim to please, Mama.

I did not finish until after my supper of blackberry jam–a finger full of which I shared with the mice by smearing it on the edge of their nest. I wrapped my blanket around me, native style, and felt as cozy and satisfied as I hoped the baby mice felt in their nest. I was especially pleased that there proved to be so many rag squares that I would be able to sleep under a double layer of adjoined scraps.

"Does life get any better than this?" I asked the dirt walls.

By the time I had swallowed a second jar of applesauce (it was a bit easier on my insides than the other fruit), the temperature had plummeted. A wicked autumnal frost was spreading over Western Oregon like a contagion, and I huddled under my quilt, where sleep made soft inroads into my consciousness.

Come back and warm me, I whispered, hoping to conjure the memory of my mother, warming me in my bed after I had a nightmare. Though she had not come in response to my conjuring her with my *mind-paintings,* still I crooned, *Come back and warm me.*

Huddle under my blanket, children. Hide from the Cold Wind brothers, answered the native mother, and I imagined myself comforted in her deep lap, anticipating one of her warming stories.

We don't play with imaginary children, I heard my own mother say.

That's only my memory of you talking, Mama. I am dreaming of my other mother now.

On some level (clearly, a loony one), I had begun to believe that dreaming of how the Warm Wind hero saved his tribe would save me too. I clenched my eyes closed and tried to reenter my dream of the Warm Wind warrior. Snuggling deeper into my oil-rag quilt, I imagined it was a voluminous skirt of turquoise, yellow, red and brown. The colors did not warm me as an electric blanket would have done, but I did not notice. And, for a time I was a member of the tribe of the Warm Wind and possessed the happy fortune of finding warm weather wherever I set up camp. If I could mind-paint the Warm Wind hero flying down out of that feathery cloud in my *Silver Thaw* picture, driven by a warming wind, he could warm the air around me, and my body. He could unfreeze my mind.

But the cold, pressing me all over, inching into my flesh, kept me from falling back asleep. I was being run over by a steamroller of cold, shaken up in a cocktail shaker of tiny cubes, pummeled with the frozen leaden boxing gloves of the Heavyweight Champ of Cold. I screamed inside, demanding that my unconscious mind hurry to the part of the tale where the Warm Wind warrior saves his tribe. But no savior arrived. My teeth were chattering like hail falling on tin and I was hanging on the tag ends of desperate. In sympathy with the Warm Wind people, I shivered on the edge of sleep. Pulling my knees to my chin and tucking my arms as far into my belly as I could, I tried to be a native mother and climb inside my own lap for warmth. When that other mother told of another of the many invasions of the Cold Wind tribe turning their warm campground to ice, I pulled my rag blanket closer around my shoulders as if it were a thick Navajo blanket. Though I imagined I was sheltering in the native mother's lap, I remained imbedded in the day of the silver thaw. And, before the Warm Wind hero could perform his deeds and finish the tale, I awoke, cold as a metal Popsicle.

I clawed my scant blanket away from my neck believing it was that too-small red snowsuit my mother had dressed me in for her photo of the silver thaw. For a moment, I was certain the Cold Wind tribe had frozen the moisture in my throat and that I was about to choke to death. I tried to scream, but could not even breathe. Realizing I lay uncovered in a cold place, I clutched at the air around me searching for my cozy bedding. I pawed at the workbench, and sought again for my lavender satin comforter, my white thermal blanket, and the flannel sheets of my marital bed, but did not find them.

Come on, Larry, don't hog all the covers.

Frantic, I almost rolled off the workbench, but, when I felt the hard wooden edge of what I had thought was my inner-spring mattress, my eyes flew open and my hopes for warmth fell to earth. Desperate to orient myself, I looked around me for clues, but dawn was trudging up over the Eastern seaboard at such a slow pace that only the window vent was visible to me.

Oh. The cellar.

As soon as I knew where I was, I felt the chill tenfold.

Had to wear your thinnest dress to entice your husband, didn't you? I've heard of dying for love, but freezing for lust?

I searched the bench for my oil-rag blanket, which had fallen to the floor. I hung down like an acrobat, clawing around in the dirt until I located one edge of the bogus blanket and drew it hand over hand to the bench top. I made myself into the tiniest ball possible, wrapped the rag blanket around me, and tucked myself into it.

I was right back in my own Ice Age, shivering with a cold as frightening as that day of the silver thaw.

Trying to invoke the native mother's voice again, I wriggled my way farther into the story of the warm wind brothers, where I hoped to spot a sign that might teach me how to ward off the cold.

The Warm Wind hero eventually learned to defeat the Cold Wind brothers. Why can't I? My fantasy turned out to be dangerous considering my current situation. All five of those icy braves came to life, slithered into the cellar, and began doing a war dance round and round on the dirt floor, turning the mud to a rink of ice. I was sure I was not hallucinating, but whatever extreme form of imagination I was exercising, it must have been the next worst thing to delusion. Those dancers were as real as the face that had looked down into mine the other night when I was dreaming in my own warm bed. Only, these braves did not dissolve into dust motes when I spoke aloud.

"Go north, and take your cold weather with you! You've arrived too early for winter."

The hand I stuck outside my blanket to shoo them away got so numb I could not feel the air moving out of the way as I pushed my palm through it. I called for aid from my mother, my father, my husband, even my in-laws, but the Cold Wind warriors kept on dancing. And the Warm Wind hero was nowhere in sight.

If this were a movie, some hero would save me.

There was that movie I saw as a kid–what was it? The one with the people trapped in a mine cave-in? That's the one Jan Sterling was in–or was it Sterling Hayden? No, it was Jan Sterling. I think there was some stolen loot involved in that movie too. Must have been a big theme in 1940s or '50s movies. *Treasure of the Sierra Madre* and all. What was it called? *Hot* something? Two words? Maybe three. *Trapped?* No. *Fire Down Below?* No, that's Rita Hayworth. Not the same kind of predicament at all. The name of that movie was bombarding the back of my memory. *Cave-In?* WHAT was it? I see Jan Sterling looking up out of the hole or down into it with those bug eyes.

In this hole, the bug-eyes are looking at me. I shivered to think how many hundreds of bug and rodent eyes must be looking at me that moment.

Ace in the Hole! That was the name of the movie with Jan Sterling--with Dan Duryea? Richard Widmark? Some slender blond actor. Kirk Douglas? Who cares anyway? They were just acting. I was the real ace in the hole.

Sleep formed only a tissue-thin coverlet over me, and I drifted in and out of consciousness. Trying hard to hold onto the idea I could mind-paint my way through this disaster, I held my one good carpenter's nail in my painting hand as if I were grasping a brush. As *Silver Thaw's* outlines sketched themselves in my head, my mind slipped--one pictorial detail at a time--into a memory that was more like a dream. I dabbed at the cold air outside my blanket, but could not get the scene to come to life. All I evoked was the memory of my charred *Silver Thaw* in our burning barrel crackling on the inner surface of my mind.

We don't want this between us, Kory.

The sudden sadness was a full-body pain. *Losing Larry.* My stomach heaved at the thought. Lurching to a sitting position, I tried not to cry. Could not afford the dehydration.

Who tried to paint this?

Rumble, rumble went my tummy as I slid off the workbench and careened across the cellar floor to relieve myself.

Gramma Moses on drugs create this mess?

The sound of the faceless frame-shop man's laughter in my head echoed the loud rumbling in my belly. In his honor, I filled another jar and staggered back to my workbench where I curled up in a corner as if frozen there.

You've been brought down out of your watercolor clouds now, daughter.

Wrong, Mama. I paint with oils.

I was but a naked body imprisoned in dirt--my dwelling a cold grave regularly befouled by its chief resident. I was horrified.

I have diarrhea of the body and constipation of the mind.

I laughed as I crossed the room to fill another jar. I thought I would not make it back to my bench. My head, muddied with the sewage of the past (not to mention the sewage of the present), clogged up and I became unable to think a clear thought or envision a creative act. I was pretty sure I would never have the energy or the clarity to paint again.

With great effort, I climbed back up onto my workbench, and then sat there open-mouthed awaiting the apprehension of a single creative notion. Each time I would recall where I was, my mouth would be dry as shredded paper and my right hand raised before me, the cramped fingers grasping an imaginary brush. Whether I had been daubing pixie paint on a dogwood blossom or blood purple on a hyacinth, I could not recall. Even my mind-painting had failed me. I felt the cellar squeezing me again, rendering me too numb to produce so much as a thumbnail sketch in the dirt wall.

Struggling to a sitting position and wrapping my quilt tight around me, I gazed across the dirt floor at the impressive pyramid of jars I had stacked in the corner farthest from my workbench. The very sight suggested I enjoy another episode of my latest hobby, perching over Mason jars. As I hunkered there, a thin slice of sunlight coming through the crack around the door struck the top jar on the pyramid, causing the glass to glow red as a votive candle holder. I felt a sudden stab of dismay when I realized that the reason for the brilliant ruby color of the jar was that it contained my blood. I nearly cried, realizing I would have to sacrifice one corner of my blanket to use as a sanitary pad. Well, not sanitary, but, I supposed sitting on a little motor oil would not hurt me. The thought made me laugh. Laughter cleared my mind long enough for me to realize shredded newspaper over a pad of paper would do me better than an oil rag. The thought made me laugh the more.

Would you MIT geniuses have thought of using newspaper for that?

I knew I was anemic, dehydrated and not a little hysterical. The stress caused by giving in to the horror of my circumstance was, I supposed, the cause of the superfluous flow I was experiencing. Physical stress combined with mental stress sometimes caused me to flow excessively. *Must consume more canned fruit.*

What? Eat more stomach-upsetting food?

No. Need more empty jars.

The cramping in my stomach made me wish some efficient angel would infuse himself into the cellar--like Zeus insinuating his seed into Danae's underground prison--and take me out of a life which had become synonymous with pain.

Danae! In a burst of radiant light, a sunbeam split into a spray of all the colors of the spectrum and coalesced in my mind into a vision of the classic case of live familial burial. Danae, Athenian princess, caught by the painter's brush at the moment she realizes she has been entombed alive by her own father. The look on her face as she takes in the great bronze ceiling meant to keep the rapist Zeus out, the velvety tapestries of a myriad of rich hues to hide the dirt walls of her grave. The only light comes from the face of the frightened girl and one oil lamp, but that light sends living threads of color to everything in her prison and makes it beautiful. A reed platter of gorgeous fruits cannot tempt her. An intricate bronze flagon of rich wine makes her sick. She wants only her plump mother's embrace, her brother's rumbling voice, the paddling fingers of free air on her cheeks. She wants to spit in her father's face. How could he imagine she would let the amorous god get near enough to harm her? And she yearns with her whole heart for Zeus not to exist.

Promising myself to paint Danae's picture as soon as I had replaced *Silver Thaw*, I spoke to Larry aloud:

"Now that was an interment, Mister! They knew how to inter a woman alive back in the Golden Age of Greece. Oh, the amenities! The viands, the rich comforts you did not afford me but which I will paint in the self-portrait I will call *Like Danae*."

It's just a week at home, Sweetie. It ain't the Bataan--.

"Oh, what would you know about it, Larry?" I muttered.

Living in Salmon Run, surrounded by community values which I found abhorrent, and yet, unable or unwilling to come out publicly against them, I saw that I was insignificant--nearly invisible--in my world. With an offer in hand to mount a worthwhile show of my paintings, I had come close to becoming myself. But, now the cellar walls were thickening, almost audibly, and soon would quash my longing for significance. And, when the walls collapsed–even if the dirt did not smother me--the house, deprived of its earthen support, would fall on me and crush me. And all the mind-paintings I had inside would be pulverized with me.

Ah, come on, Kory, people have been kidnaped and held in solitary, in smaller, dirtier, colder cells than yours.

That was Larry-in-my-head reminding me, as he often did, that I was fortunate to be a pampered American woman.

You're free, white and twenty-one, Kory.

That doesn't mean I can't aspire to a fuller humanity than I can now claim, Larry.

You have food, and a roof over your head.

Larry was right: I had a roof and a floor over my head. Fortunate woman. And yet I had come to this: spending every moment in regret, anger and blame. And fear of being smothered and pressed to a smudge.

The majority of the people in the world don't have it as soft as you do, Kory.

Then why am I lying on a hard bench, Larry?

I could feel fever spreading through me, and every time it spiked, the Cold Wind warriors resumed their dance. The aura around them was an alarming silver color that made me tremble. And, when I began to shiver, the coughing began. It came from deep down on my right side and it hurt like hell. Straining to suppress the next cough, I still tried to complete the painting in my mind before anything worse happened to me. I gave a sharp laugh.

The consumptive artiste dying in the garret.

Larry put in his comment as usual.

Aw, come on, Kory, you lost a painting, not an ear like Van Gogh.

When you let that cellar door drop, I lost more than a painting.

I huddled in the middle of my workbench in as small a ball as I could make of myself. With my arms crossed over my bowed head, I protected the back of my skull from the tons of earth and lumber I was certain would crash down on me momentarily. I felt the impact of immense dirt slabs on my skin, on my flesh, and my bones. I believed cold earth would cover me in an instant. I forgot who I was, where I came from, how I spent my time, whom I knew. Whoever I was, I would rather be dead then to feel the awful pressure of being flattened and asphyxiated.

In my weakening state, I stared dully at the rich red color gleaming in the top jar of my pyramid. I had always found the color of this blood beautiful– like ripe cherries only with more sunshine in the red. A surge of artistic longing flowed through me, an impression of color and other memories straining to reach the easel through me. My painting hung in mid-air, where an aura of dust motes made my hand glow as if filled with light.

The brush flows towards the waiting canvas.

I closed my eyes and, for the hundredth time, tried to imagine the first stroke my brush would make on *Silver Thaw* when once I ascended to my sunroom studio.

That is how I will save myself.

I would show those Cold Wind brothers how the Warm Wind hero swept down from the sky and brought summer to the land.

The easel unfolds, its joints creaking like splintered bones.

I forced myself to sit up on my workbench, raised my hand as if it held a brush, and tried to flap my fingers the way I imagined I once had done.

First, I would paint the little braves sliding down the sandy slope in their oval dishpan. Wonderful sunlight would infuse the scene across the river. The laughing native mother sitting cross-legged on a blanket on the warm sandy riverbank.   I began daubing a rainbow of colors into the deep black troughs of the waves in the center of the river, and was congratulating myself for repainting *Silver Thaw*.   Then I was handing my completed *Women of Myth* collection over to the gallery owner, saying, "Here is the star of my nine-day *oeuvre*," when a familiar voice hooted in my head.

Oeuvre, OEUVRE! Larry cackled.   *Who do you think you are, the poor man's Gramma Moses?*

The easel unfolds....

And his laughing voice:

Gramma Moses' oeuvre, forsooth!

That sent me on another trip across that dirt floor, but there were no empty jars available. Forced by the sharp cramping in my belly to choose fast, I found a spot where the dirt was crumbled enough that I could scrape

Two Mothers

Something woke me. I raised my head, hoping I had heard the noise of young laughter, of splashing water, of stones skipping on a wet surface.

Scamps?

I reached my hand to my face to brush something off of my cheek. It was not a party of worms playing pinochle on my snout as I had feared. I had been moaning and groaning for so long that my tears had formed a mud puddle beneath my face, leaving earth caked on me from temple to chin. I pushed myself up to the length of my arms and realized I was lying on the cellar floor in wet dirt.

"Mud," I whispered, proud of my perceptive powers. I was so spent from fighting the cold, and from coughing that I had evidently not made it back to the workbench from my litter box the last time. I scooped up a finger full of mud and held it close to my eyes. I could not see it well in that light, but needed to confront it, in order to think something through.

Momentarily I wondered whether I was in the monster in the riverbank's hole. Across from the little braves' swimming hole. I did not hear them my last morning above ground, but they only come in the late afternoon, after picking beans all day down by the Columbia.

Certain now that I must have heard them playing in the river below the orchard when I first woke, I called out to them.

"At least you scamps might hear me. Come save me, scamps." I roused myself and somehow managed to crawl back onto the workbench and clap two jar lids together. "Scamps! Wild Indians? Little braves, I want to paint you!"

I had saved one of them once. She would be a teenager now. Not too old to take a swim in her family's favorite swimming hole.

At that moment on that final day in the cellar, hearing sounds floating uphill from the river, the moment that had inspired the painting I had avoided painting for decades flooded my mind again. For the one picture I wanted most to paint was not my painting of the coldest day I had known. Its theme would be the prime motif of *Women of Myth,* feminine strength emerging, not from the ownership of land, but from the earth itself. Too sick and exhausted to resist, at last I faced the memory of a slim arm reaching out of the sand.

The elements of the painting come unbidden: the little braves leaping high in the air over the Silky, the sun over the cottonwoods painting the boys gold against a fiery sky, the river still dark as ink beneath them, and the colors of their mother's skirts, swirling, dissolving in the river. Raising her vivid blanket above her shoulders like eagle wings, she tries to fly to the aid of the girl who is swimming toward my side of the river where the monster waits. Only, that one native girl has strayed from the happy group. My eye caught her in the moment when she first plunged into the water. I feel a burgeoning frustration that I cannot run to my sunroom to paint her, but I tamp it down and double my resolve to paint her the only way I can in my dark cellar room.

The easel opens, bleeding marrow. The brush flows to my hand. Paint to canvas.

That fine morning long ago when I was home on holiday from college--that day when my mother had run down the lane to the river shouting *Scamps* and found the mother of the Native American children shouting to my mother from the opposite riverbank. *Help, Missus! Help, Missus!* And my mother running faster and faster till she was a blur.

The monster at the bottom of the orchard is after the braves!

I ran from the picnic table in the north meadow where I was painting a watercolor of Mt. Hood in twenty shades of white. The clashing of the two women's voices mingling with the sound of the rapids above the orchard was terrifying, but, in the face of all that caterwauling, a college girl like me, home from art school for the summer, could not be expected to stay away from the orchard and the terror beyond. Though Mama had run down the lane, I took the short cut to the Indian mother through the forbidden apple trees as I had so many times dreamed I would do. Yellow jackets covered the windfall apples like a live carpet of gold and I alternately ran and hopped my way down to the riverbank to avoid being stung or tripped up by the tangle of deadwood from the aged trees. A swath of the bees flew behind me through the orchard like a long golden scarf flying in the wind.

The first thing I saw through the trees was several small children jumping up and down across the river. Their mother was struggling toward our side of the river, her voluminous cotton skirts billowing around her. The river was not deep at that time of year, but it was treacherously swift. And the woman's fight against the current was doubled by her fight against her encumbering skirts.

The first thing I saw as I burst out of the trees, was my own mother struggling through the blackberry vines which separated the lane from the riverbank just south of the orchard. Then she was rounding the corner of the orchard and roaring along the sandy shore. I never would have imagined she could walk through blackberry vines or that she could move that fast. Her apron clung to her body, revealing her plump middle-age belly, and her hands clawed the air before her as if she could pull herself along faster that way. Though I reached the site of the disaster before she did--and long before the mother of the child in distress half-swam and half-trudged across the river–I stopped for a long moment attempting to take in the scene. I could not readily parse its meaning.

Expecting to find myself atop the high river bank of my nightmares, I found myself standing on a flat beach choked with mud and odd grasses. And, in the middle of the lush flat land was half a child–happily it was a living half, though a terrified one. The girl had sunk to her waist in a patch of the super-saturated soil called quicksand. The monster I had been forbidden to approach all my life did not dwell in a riverbank cave but in a deep pot of clinging, sucking, fluid sand. By the time I made my brain reorganize and accept the true view of the riverbank, the girl's flailing and squirming had driven her farther down into the sand until it was lapping slow motion at her chest.

"Lie flat on your back and float!" my mother shouted as she sailed down the shore.

The little girl only squirmed more wildly in her panic. She was facing away from her mother in the river and towards me as she cried, "Ma! Ma!" The expression on her face will be with me forever. That little face shocked me out of my frozen state and I ran back into the woods. The children across the water screamed, "No, No! Come back, Miss!" The mother cried out to me, too, as she approached shore and tried to pull herself and her drenched skirt out of the river. Her moccasins kept slipping on the slimy round stones in the shallows as she tried to gain her footing. My own mother cried my name, whether to warn me away from the quicksand one more time or to call me back to save the girl, I did not know. I picked up two large branches I had jumped over at the edge of the woods. The yellow jackets whirled around with me as I turned back to the river. Some of them stung me but I did not know it at the time. They stung the little girl and my mother too as I threw myself flat beside Mama and handed her one of the branches. When we reached them towards the girl, she grabbed them with a death grip.

"Float on your belly!" Mama urged her. She must have thought what to say and do many times in case I had ever made my way to the riverbank and fell in. I could not imagine at that time--though I understood later when I was in her same situation--what anguish she must have gone through, imagining every day that I might end up like this little girl. "Don't wriggle, sweetheart. Let us pull you. You're all right now. You're going to be all right. Let yourself go. We'll pull you."

Inch by inch we tugged her toward solid ground. Every Thanksgiving my mother used to say that the hardest task in the world was to pull the giblet packet out of the nether maw of a frozen turkey carcass. She never said it again after we worked to pull that little girl out of the hazard which one old geezer of the town once called Mother Nature's asshole. The ancient apple branch that Mama held cracked and split and the girl's little hand reached out towards my Mama's as if to wave goodbye. I pulled my branch with frantic tugs, but the earth held on to the girl's slender body. The sucking sand seemed a living malevolent thing. I was only vaguely aware that I was facing my dream monster in its riverbank cave. I dropped my branch and reached out to grab the girl's forearms. My chin and chest broke the surface of the sand puddle and I could feel its terrible power sucking at my breasts. To keep from falling nose first into the slime, I gave a mighty jerk backwards, pulling the child with me. At the same time, Mama pushed herself to her knees and, as I pulled, she pushed at the girl's waist and buttocks until she was all the way out of the quicksand. With the child tucked into my lap, I rolled over then handed the child to Mama who wrapped her in her apron. The girl's mother crawled up onto the sand and knelt beside her girl. Together the two mothers carried her down to the river and washed her in a miniature bay formed between two low boulders. I followed and washed my arms and splashed my chest and face with water.

"Tell your children to stay where they are," my mother told the woman. "I'll drive you and your girl around by the bridge and pick them up. We'll take the child to the doctor together."

The woman nodded numbly. She was freezing cold herself, I could see, though it was a warm day. She was calling instructions to her children across the river as I ran up to the house, got the keys to Mama's Plymouth

163

and drove it down the lane to pick up Mama and the native mother and child. Standing knee deep in the river at the foot of the blackberry vine, we formed a bucket brigade and handed the girl from one to the other until I had her in my arms and put her in the car. I got Daddy's old wool Navy blanket out of the trunk and wrapped it around her in the back seat. After the two mothers had climbed in on either side of the girl, I drove them down River Road to Goat's Bridge, crossed over to the Silky Road and sped to the farm across the river from our house. The girl's mother seemed to scrunch down as we passed the farmer in his field. I supposed she was used to sneaking along the river bank to get to the swimming hole and did not want him to see her. She and my mother held the girl between them in the back seat and rubbed her legs and arms to warm her. They would pull a leg or arm out from beneath the wool blanket and rub it until it was warmer and then cover it again before they pulled out another limb to warm it. When we picked up the other children, the woman actually counted heads before we started for the doctor's office. I thought what a good mother she must be to avoid the kind of common panic that allows an accident to happen to a second child when a parent is tending to the mischance of the first one.

    In all the time when we were rescuing the child, taking her to the doctor's office, and driving her and the rest of her family back to their home–an abandoned mustard-colored railroad repair cabin above the tracks just east of the bridge–the Native American woman never said a word of blame to my mother or about suing my parents for not preventing such a horrible misstep by an unwitting trespasser. I was amazed that she did not turn to my mother, give her a stern look and say, "You trespass on our land, and then you do not make it safe." But, if she was blaming anyone, I felt, it was not the odious philosophy of Manifest Destiny. She seemed to be blaming herself for allowing her children to trespass. I thought possibly that, as an original possessor of the land, a Native American might believe that the land itself was responsible for both the riches it offers us and the dangers with which it challenges us. But, really, what struck me beyond thoughts of liability or Daddy's lawyer were the two mothers--my forbidding Norwegian American mama and her amiable Native American counterpart--working together to calm and warm a frightened little girl. Of my own mother, I thought: *The woman's immersed in triteness, yet she can rise to magnificence at need.*

That night my father said he would have the patches of quicksand filled with boulders, and I slept without a hint of the nightmare that had plagued me all my young life. When the property had passed from my parents to me, therefore, I did not worry about the quicksand. I did ask about it, but Daddy's attorney took Larry aside and spoke to him about it when I was signing the ownership papers with my parents. Later I found out that he figured I would have the same objections as my mother, and advised Larry to lead me to believe he had dealt with the quicksand. *I told you I'd take care of it. Relax! Have a little trust, Kory.*

When I had helped pull the little girl from the quicksand, I had ended up swollen from head to foot with bee stings which took long uncomfortable days to heal. As a result, I had such a horror of that insect-infested orchard that I had not walked down through it to verify his claim that he had filled in the quicksand pots. I admit too that, after the monster's roar had returned to my dreams, the orchard was still so taboo to me that I never walked through it to explore that stretch of the riverbank.

Lying on my unforgiving bench in the cellar I could smell fruit and sugar water which had soaked into the mud floor, and the hint of blood-soaked newsprint which I had been too weak to cover with mud. I was thinking about my father's cry of liability and my mother's counter-cry *morally-at-fault*. Both terms smelled worse than the cellar to me. *I ought to have checked.* Before I signed those ownership papers, and especially, with a young adventurous child in the house, I certainly ought to have walked down below the orchard to check the place where I believed the quicksand had been eliminated. But, ignorance is a flimsy door to hide behind.

I had done nothing about the quicksand until last week, when I had found out the reason for the feud between the Nakamuras and the Stamps. Then I had told Larry I wanted to have that whole rotting orchard renovated so someone could put the land to good use.

"Nakamura, you mean," Larry had snorted.

No more about that, I told my memory. I had just heard someone splashing and laughing in the river below the orchard, hadn't I? I imagined the river across from the orchard filled with leaping little braves, and I smiled. It was too cool for me in the cellar today, but the sun shone hot outside and the air was still. A perfect fall swimming day. I hoped the little girl we saved was in the mood for a swim. But she might be too old now to play in the river. Perhaps her children? Stranger coincidences have occurred in the world.

After devoting my energies to coughing for a quarter hour, I pulled myself up to the window grill, knelt on my quilt and began calling to the girl I had helped save years ago. But my voice sounded like the crackling of a small fire. "Help!" came out as more of a croak. I had shouted so long and hard at the implacable cosmos that I did not have the voice to call out to real people who could be swimming within reach of my voice. And, I was almost certain I could hear them now, splashing one another, sputtering with laughter as they surfaced for air. "Help me!" I cried. No reply. No sound of little bare feet running across the shallows, pounding up the dusty path to the house.

Wouldn't the Silky's babbling drown out my cries anyway? How many yards uphill from the swimming hole is the house? I closed my eyes and counted on my fingers. How long was the rutted track to the river? Each gooseberry bush along that lane was how wide? I stood next to one in my mind and noted how far I had to reach right and left to pick the berries at the extreme edges of the bush. Maybe three to four feet wide. How far between bushes? How many bushes running from river to house? However hopefully I calculated the distance from my shouts to the children's ears, it was a long way. And, the orchard and the leviathan blackberry vine lay between the swimming hole and the house--all those rotting trees still covered with blighted leaves and squishy apples would even absorb the cries of a great grizzly with her paw caught in a bear trap.

I calculated that the youngsters could have heard me if they were within reach of my normal voice. But, the Native American scout with the keenest hearing known to the Columbia River tribes could not hear my cries now–not if he or she had his ear pressed to the window grill seven feet from me. "How can I expect the little braves swimming down below the orchard to hear me?" I rasped. I resumed croaking like an underground frog, though I was sure no one but the beetles under the workbench could hear me, and maybe the monster in the riverbank–which doesn't even exist except in my dreams. Unlike all the other folks inhabiting my immediate world, the braves were regular visitors from whom I expected nothing. Yet, somehow, of all the people who might have happened by, they were the ones I hoped might come by again and save me. With effort, I climbed onto my usual perch and lay with my cheek on the oily wood of the workbench, forming a movie in my mind of the *wild Indians* taking pity on the caged white woman and freeing her. Fascinated since childhood by the symbolic elements of the Indian mother's stories, I felt rather than believed I had maintained some sort of unspoken spiritual connection with the family over the years. Such an unwarranted mystical expectation I had about them.

Ah, Kory, what a sentimental image you have of the rapscallions who lusted after our apples.

Your voice has lost its hold on me, Larry. It's just a memory without muscle.

Though the shriveling voice of reason deep inside

me counselled me otherwise, the feeling that the Native American children would save me somehow soothed me, and I dozed, I do not know how long. I lurched awake only when I heard a noise.

My voice had returned after rest several times, but the last time it disappeared--when I was yelling at Larry-in-my-head--it did not return. Now my voice was about as far gone as Larry's imaginary one, but I could still rattle and bang on the wire vent cover with my jar lids. Bang, bang, bang and three long scrapes, metal on metal. Did Native Americans know about Morse code? *Listen.* No running feet coming up the lane–bare feet on dust and pebbles. *I must have imagined I heard them.* I feared the little braves had better things to do than swim that day. Probably picking huckleberries or pine nuts to help support the family. Reluctantly, I lay aside my jar lids as I added my phantom wild Indian playmates to my long list of people who had disappointed me.

But, though my body and my voice were used up, enough mental gristle remained to make me reach up to the head of my wooden bed where I kept my two metal Kerr lids. I held one metal lid in each hand whenever I lay down. It would be only fitting to hang on to them this one last time. If I were to wake to the sound of anyone passing, I would bang them together or drag them across the window grill.

❧

The Farmer

I lay there on the workbench with my jar lids gripped in my sweaty hands, drifting in and out of a fevered sleep. Crowds of people and ancient incidents strolled in and out of my skull, chatting about events just witnessed, episodes upcoming, tragedies momently unfolding. And, at the peak of this multifarious drama, I realized I was supposed to step on stage any moment in the role of Amaterasu. Yet I could not remember a single one of my lines. Obviously, the setting was the cave in which the Japanese goddess hid from her brother, the storm god. But, I could not be Amaterasu: I was not mad at my brother. I had no brother. There was no denying that I was in a cave for some reason though. Nicky appeared at the mouth of the cave and tried to explain all the fuss and fury of characters moving about in the dark, but, though I could somehow see his lips move in the gloom and trace with my finger the concern on his face, I could not hear his words. Still I touched his face in air with my hand, anticipating with delight that he had said I could paint him soon. But, an endless holiday party was going on in the hallowed house of old events in my mind and I kept losing hold of the tail of my last thought. What part was I expected to play in the story of the lady in a cave? I caught only shreds of the dialogues being rehearsed around me, until a comment by a distant neighbor, or a single word, *scamps*, would pull the string on a memory long forgotten, which would then play itself out beneath my eyelids.

My present situation would rise to the surface now and then to assure me that death by anemia would be peaceful--all soft humming in the ears, in the limbs, in the digits, like the soothing hands of a goddess, I supposed, vibrating on the skin, or, to be honest, the hands of my mother on one of her best days when I was small.

Scamps!

There it was again, the trigger word of that final

morning. I had heard it upon waking. Had I really called out to the swimming children? Or, had I merely heard the word *scamps* and dreamed I was awake and calling to them? The voice belonged to my mother--you could not have convinced anyone else to claim that voice, so unsure of pitch and so sure of her tried-and-true opinions. Well, tried; not necessarily true.

Just last week when Nicky Nakamura had inquired about pulling up the old fruit trees, I had felt a great surge of relief welling up inside me. I had been willing, but my discussion with Larry–if you can call two people moving from room to room around their house scowling and avoiding eye contact a discussion–was not, as it were, fruitful.

"Nick just wants to get his paws on my stuff," Larry had joked.

"Who would want to get his hands on those trees? They are a blight."

"You said those trees were picturesque," he reminded me.

"Our son's safety would be more beautiful," was basically all I said.

"It's your job to keep an eye on the scamp," was his final word on the subject.

The scamp!

Lying locked in the cellar, I heard the word again, only this time I was able to rouse myself enough to note that it was a man's voice--neither my mother's, nor Larry's--calling, "Scamp!" A raspy old-sounding man's voice, like Nicky Nakamura's foreman, the homeless man he picked up by the underpass downtown where jobless men sleep at night and wait for farm employment in the early mornings. Jimmy was his name and Nicky had kept him on because, though I secretly suspected he spent the off-season drinking something horrid on a blown-out mattress under an overpass in downtown Riverport, he was a loyal, tireless worker from planting through harvest time. Cozy in my rag comforter, all my surfaces humming, hinting of the ultimate comforts of the next world, I did not want to think about Nicky's foreman for whom a cozy workbench bed in his own cellar out of the wind and cold might well seem heaven compared to the underpass where he spent his winters. I burrowed deeper into my blanket.

"Mrs. Scamp!" he cried, closer now. "Hey Missus! Mrs. Scamp!"

Could Jimmy be calling to the mother of the swimming children? No, her name couldn't be Mrs. Scamp. That was only my mother's epithet for the Indian children.

"Mrs. Stamp!" the gravelly voice shouted, and I sat straight up on my bench. A wave of dizziness pitched my head sideways against the cold concrete foundation. Sleep had returned enough strength to me that I was able to right myself again and search for my two metal jar lid castanets. I reached up on the window ledge for them under the vent hole, on the end of the workbench. *Not there!* I scrabbled wildly in the folds of my oil-rag comforter and finally found them in my own hands. I had been gripping them so hard all night that the rims had worked their way into the flesh of my palms. With probably the greatest effort I would make in my life, I pushed myself upright and began to bang the lids against the wire window grating.

"Here I am," I cried, again and again, with all the volume of one of those sad dogs who has had his vocal cords cut. My cry sounded to my ears more like, "Heh ahem!" all breath and no vocal chords. But, I played my castanets for all I was worth–which, admittedly, was not much at that point.

The man, though, heard the clatter of the jar lids. Bless the winos of the world, I thought, as Jimmy came into sight around the side of the house. Where was his scraggly beard though, or his dry, red-rimmed eyes? He was clean-shaven as a bank teller. Never had a man looked so appealing to me. I would have dated him if he had asked me. I kept clapping metal against metal. Why had I not done that days ago when my father came by?

171

Why had I taken that moment to nap away my freedom?

Jimmy shouted down into my wire grating, "Mrs. Stamp. I got to use your phone. My boss's boy is up ta' his hips in river bank."

I mouthed some answer.

"Please, ma'am. Don't mean ta' bother ya', but we need ta' call the fire truck."

I clicked my lids on the screen.

"Ma'am, I'm using your phone whether you say so or no." The words were wrenched out of a man obviously used to avoiding stepping on the toes of people who live in houses and eat regular meals. He ran around to the back of the house and I forced myself to stumble to the cellar door. I could not pound on it, but I managed to pull my father's red hanky from my pocket and used my big nail to poke it up through the crack around the door.

"Oh!" he said, and, stringy and ill-nourished as he was, he managed to pull out the padlock, tug up the latch and wrench the door open. It crashed against its supporting tree stump with a clap like thunder and the parts of it not reinforced with iron splintered and fell into the gladiola bed. Jimmy came running down the stairs, and, taking in the scene in a split-second, picked me up without so much as a grimace of disgust at my condition. I suppose he had seen much worst sights living in the back alleys of downtown Riverport. He ran up the stairs with me in his arms as easily as if I were a rag doll he had found in a gutter somewhere. I would not have thought those skinny arms could have such steely muscles in them.

"Oh!" I rasped, seeing my yard for the first time in what seemed more like nine months than nine days, "The snow's all melted." It seemed the right thing to say at the time.

"What?" Jimmy muttered, as he carried me to the kitchen door.

"The silver has all thawed," I murmured as he lowered my feet to the sidewalk. I was embarrassed that

I was not able to talk sense. My head was in another language.

Jimmy supported me with one arm while he tried the back door with the other. Thinking of Nicky's sweet two year old son who sometimes played with my Bertie on the schoolyard swings on weekends, I was filled with panic and frustration. Why would the door not open for us? Larry must have locked the back porch. Making sure his tools and all his other belongings were bolted up tight before he left. I knocked on Jimmy's shoulder with one of my jar lids and then tapped on the window of the door with it. I was too weak to break the window myself, but he understood my meaning and, taking the lid from my hand, used it to punch out the window. With the arm that was not supporting me, he pulled out the jagged glass and reached in to open the door. He dragged me into the house and I pointed to the kitchen wall phone. He laid me on the kitchen table and I let my head fall on my outstretched arm while he phoned the operator and asked her to send the rescue squad.

"Tell Mama to bring my snowsuit," I squeaked. "Everything's melted, but I'm still cold."

By the time the firemen arrived, Nicky had managed to pull his son from the quicksand and brought him to the house. When Larry had told him "we" would consider renting some land to him, he had neglected to tell him about the quicksand and the quicksand had no longer existed in my mind. Nicky told me later that he had taken his boy and Jimmy with him to look at the orchard. Hank had strayed a few yards away from the two men and stumbled into a pit of quicksand. I indicated to Nicky by means of limp gestures that I had thought the quicksand had been filled in with boulders years before. Nick gave me a strange look, and I realized I had just revealed that someone had failed to make the riverbank safe as promised.

Somehow Nick found towels, warm water, soap, a blanket– whatever he needed to make his boy comfortable. He had Jimmy find a warm blanket and wrap me in it. Then I let my head fall back onto the kitchen table where it landed with the sound of a temple gong.

I kept hearing bells and wished my head would stop ringing, but Jimmy put a hand on my shoulder and asked, "Want me to get the phone, ma'am?" Turning my head so that I could look up at him with one eye, I gave him the most beseeching look I could manage on short notice. "Okay," he drawled, as if to say, "They'll know it's a seasonally recovered wino by the sound of my whiskey tenor, but I'll do it if you want."

Not blessed with a continual state of consciousness, I did not catch much of his conversation, but, from what Jimmy reported to me during one of my waking moments, the fire truck had made it halfway down River Road, before it hit the one sharp curve in the road at top speed, whereupon the right front wheel struck a sinkhole on the shoulder and sank up to the rim top.

"Quicksand's spreading!" I raised my head to rasp. "Everybody up the bluff!" I giggled once before my face merged with the kitchen table top again.

"How long? Did they say?" Nick asked Jimmy, handing a bathed and towel-wrapped Hank to him. The boy began playing with a Coke-bottle charm hanging from the zipper of Jimmy's denim jacket.

"A while," Jimmy regretted. "They radioed for a truck jack to be brought to 'em from Ten Mile Willy's. Salmon Run ain't got one."

"We'll have to do what we can for them ourselves for now. Can't leave her covered in crud like this."

He pulled my right arm over his shoulder, draped it around his neck, and scraped me off the table like a roll of pastry.

"Find some toys to amuse Hank, will you, Jimmy?" he asked.

"Things I do for my pay," Jimmy grumbled as he looked around for some toys. Before long, we could hear Hank and Jimmy laughing by Bertie's toy box.

While Nick carried me to the bathroom, I could feel my head lolling around, but had no power to lift it. My voice had been restored enough, however, that I could lift it to praise Jimmy. "He held his face up like a mirror to me, Nicky, and drew me right out of my cave. Thought the sun was never going to shine again. That guy deserves a raise."

While I babbled mostly soundlessly about how I once was the Japanese goddess Amaterasu, Nick balanced me on his lap, filled the tub, sprinkled in half a bottle of bubble bath, and then slid my soiled muumuu off over my head and tugged my pants down to the floor. Most days I would have felt humiliated by the state of me and my undies, but that day I would not have cared if the whole town had watched me bathe nude on Main Street. Nick slid me off his lap into a mound of bubbles so high I disappeared in white fluff.

"Snowing again!" I croaked. "Always comes in layers: snow, rain, thaw, freeze, and snow again. Does Bertie have his snowsuit on?" I mewled, sitting up. Then my attention was captured by the globs of bubbles that were sliding down my breasts. "I'm snowing!" I giggled.

Nicky helped me lie back in the tub. I was so giddy that the feel of water all over my body intoxicated me. The beauty and wonder of clean water filled what consciousness I had left. I felt my whole life had come to that thirst-quenching moment and I turned my face into the water and tried to drink it. When I got a mouth full of bubbles and gagged, Nick realized I could not be trusted to bathe myself. He reached through the bubbles, and raised my head with a supporting forearm.

"Poor Kory. You're about to die of thirst."

I was still trying to twist my neck to lap up some bath water when a brown hand with a glass of water touched my lips. While supporting my heavy head with his left arm, Nick had reached over to the sink and filled the bathroom glass with the best thing since the Big Bang. It was a clean jelly glass with yellow tulips painted on it, and, inside, was clear pure Mt. Hood watershed water. After I drank as much as Nick would allow, I let my head fall back on his forearm and closed my eyes. With soap on a washcloth that said *MRS.* which he found hanging on the tub rack, Nick gently washed off all the blood, crap and mud I had accumulated in the past nine days. At first the bubbles covered all, but, the cloudier the water became, the less it could support the bubbles. Still, Nick sloshed soapy water over me with one arm while supporting my neck with the other until I was clean. Nothing seemed odd or inappropriate about the scene as I experienced it--a neighbor man and old friend bathing me. I felt protected and cared for. I thought nothing odd about the foreman in the living room diverting a boy from the memory of his recent quicksand trauma, me lying limp in a bath under mounds of bubbles, and the farmer washing me with the stern objectivity with which he hosed down his cow.

When the best bath anyone ever had was over, Nick let the water out of the tub, wrapped me in one of Larry's extra-large bath towels, and supported me while I sat on the edge of the tub and let the enveloping towel dry me.

"I wish there were a woman here to help you do this, but there isn't," Nick stated without embellishment.

That made me cry, and I let out all the tears I had held in for lack of water to replenish them. I heard myself babbling about the cellar door.

"It happened on my head, crashing," I tried to explain. My voice was coming out in rasps, spit and whistles. Nick sat beside me on the edge of the tub drying my hair and my tears with a hand towel, occasionally leaning his forehead against mine to hear what I was saying.

The bathroom looked unfamiliar to me, but I knew who was drying my hair.

"Have we been interned, Nicky?" I whispered. Though I could feel my face was swollen and red from crying, I looked up at him for confirmation.

"No, Kory, you're home now. You're all right now."

I may have been mistaken, but I thought he was the one doing the crying.

"I thought Uncle Sam or Zeus or somebody like that had stuffed me in a hole in the ground," I gasped. "I'm so sorry they roped you into it too, Nicky."

"I hear the fire truck, Kory. And the ambulance. They'll take you to the hospital and get you well again."

"I don't want us to be interned," I sobbed.

"What is she talking about and what the hell do you think you're doing, Nakamura?"

When I saw Larry standing in the bathroom doorway, I shrank against Nick.

"She's just had a bath after being locked in the cellar. She was in pretty bad shape," Nick said, wrapping the towel tighter around my shoulders.

The firemen clomped into the picture in their big floppy boots. Somebody lifted me onto a Gurney and covered me with a stack of wool blankets. It was the strangest movie I ever was in. It gave me the chills, but those blankets were heaven. All the way to the ambulance parked in our driveway, I could hear men talking. A fireman came back within a minute and radioed the police. Nick whispered to another fireman, "She's bleeding very heavily."

"I saw--in the cellar," the fireman said. He turned and glanced at me sharply as if I might have a knife sticking out of my skull. "Ma'am, did you get cut or stabbed or anything down there?"

I looked up at his sweet boyish face. His blue eyes were filled with a kind of pity and concern I had never seen before. I thought if anyone could look at the whole earth in one moment with such eyes, all wounds would be healed at once.

"Not that kind of bleeding, Kenny," Nick muttered to the fireman. "She has some scrapes and splinters, but most of the blood she lost when I was helping her bathe is because it's her time."

"You *bathed* her?" Larry snarled. "You bastard!"

"She's been shut in that hole for don't know how long," Jimmy interrupted, preventing Larry from hitting Nick. "Case you get to wonderin', I had to break your back window to get to the phone."

"You broke my window? Nick, I told you not to hire that hobo scum. Kory, what's going on here?"

Larry's face appeared above mine.

"Who did this to her? You?" Larry demanded of the foreman. Jimmy looked slight as a reed in the path of a firestorm but he did not back up.

"He saved her from that mess down there," Nick said, stepping to Jimmy's side to confront Larry again. I would gladly have disappeared under the Gurney and never been seen again, to think of all the people who had seen and would see the mess I had made of the cellar.

"We'll wait while you take a look," said one of the two policemen who had arrived with the ambulance.

"You ordering me to go down cellar, Officer? My own damn cellar?"

"He means go down *to the* cellar, Officer." I giggled to think Larry would be irritated at me for putting *to the* back into our description of the cellar.

When my husband got a look at my colorful montage in the cellar, he roared like a cave bear disturbed mid-winter.

"I want to know who did this!"

I could hear him running up the concrete steps. *What a lovely thing--to run up the cellar steps and out into the night.* He stopped at the ambulance door and demanded the same thing of Nicky.

"Who the fuck did this?"

"Figure it out," said Nicky.

"Kory, what the fuck have you done?" Larry shouted into the ambulance.

"What have *you* done, Larry?" Nicky asked.

"You'd do better to ask what I *will* do when I find out who did all this damage to my house–and my wife.

Have your *workers* been squatting in my cellar? The place smells like a latrine."

"Better ask what you did *not* do," Nicky spat. I could see over my now very flat belly that he and Larry were nose to nose outside the ambulance.

"What didn't I do, farm boy?" Larry sneered.

"Leave the cellar door open, Larry," said Nick through gritted teeth. "Leave the goddam door open."

"What are you talking about?"

"Did you lock your wife in the cellar, sir?" asked a policeman who, as far as I knew, had emerged from the clouds.

"Of course not."

"She said you did," Nick and Jimmy said at once.

"She's delirious," Larry said.

"It's looking like you did...." said the policeman.

"That's ridiculous. A fly could push that door open. Kory, what have you been handing these guys?"

"Then you did shut the door on her?"

"If I had, she could have gotten out. Who would shut a door on his wife if he thought she was not strong enough to open it?"

"She says you saw her drop a tray full of jelly jars," said Nick. "Yet you thought her arms were strong enough to push open an iron-clad door?"

"She's stronger than she lets on," Larry averred.

"The lock wasn't locked, officer," said Jimmy to the policeman, "but it was looped through the hasp."

Larry was about to leap at Jimmy's throat when the paramedic began to pull the ambulance doors shut.

"Hey, where are you taking my wife?"

"To the hospital," said the paramedic. "She's dehydrated, feverish, suffering from exposure and exhaustion and probably anemia. As you may have noticed, she's got a severe cough. She needs medical attention."

"Exposure? I was sleeping outdoors on top of my sleeping bag every night and, if anything, I was too warm. She was lucky she was indoors."

"The weather has been a little cooler on this side of the mountains for the last week and a half. As a weatherman, I would think you would know that."

"I was on vacation!"

It was not a vacation! I mouthed.

"I'm going to ride in the ambulance with her," said Larry, gripping the ambulance door.

I tried to scoot away from him on the Gurney, but lacked the strength.

"You think that makes sense right now, really?"

The ambulance doors closed between me and my husband.

"I have some rights here, you know," Larry shouted, thumping the doors.

The driver took that as a *Good to go*, and started down the drive. Larry strode to the foot of the driveway. I saw him standing there, stiff with fists clenched at his sides. When he disappeared from the back window of the ambulance, we were about halfway up River Road, and I was crying for too many reasons to count. <u>Now</u>, *you're anxious to get to me, Larry.*

We passed the chief of police's car heading to our house.

Uh-oh! Something serious going on at the old homestead. Are they going to arrest the cellar?

I had to stop laughing and crying simultaneously, because it made me cough

More Than Two Cents Worth

"Told you we should have put his name on the title too."

My father's voice, and he was whispering. Then my mother, whose whisper hits like a fog full of knives:

"The theory being if we gave him as much as we gave our daughter, he would not have forgotten to leave the cellar door open?"

"A man doesn't want to feel less equal than equal, if you know what I mean," said Daddy.

"Dear, that bedpan there knows what you mean."

I'm in the hospital. I opened my eyes.

"Where am I?" I knew that even without seeing the bedpan on its stand and the IV drip and all. What I meant to say was "Why am I?" I had fainted in the ambulance and had thought the sensation of sinking into a narrowing hole under a brightening white sky meant I was dying.

"Hospital," offered my father. "Won't be here long. You're okay, just...kind of weak."

"Anemic and dehydrated, they said, and pneumonia, for heaven's sake!"

True to form, Mama scolded me with the diagnosis, as if it were my doing. I vowed never to tell her I had been barefoot and wearing a flimsy gown or I would never hear the end of it.

"Where's Bertie?"

"With your Aunt Flo. She'll meet us later at home."

"*At what home?*" I wanted to know. I was in no mood to go back to my own home just yet.

"How long since you lightened your hair?" my mother demanded, changing the subject. "You were such an adorable blonde child."

"'Bout nine days, I'm guessing, since I bleached my roots–because I was busy living among the roots." I felt a small cough creeping up from somewhere deep on the tail of my laughter.

"Daddy," I whispered in his ear, "Did you put the

181

lock in the hasp--you know, when you dropped off Larry's tool box?"

"Why would I?" he asked.

"Old habit?" The cough was getting close to my throat.

"If I did it on autopilot, I wouldn't remember, would I?"

"So, we'll never know if Larry locked me in on purpose," I nodded.

"What a morbid thought!" my mother said. "You know your husband didn't mean to overlook you that way."

"Overlook me, Mama? To me, such a huge event, can never be overlooked."

A small coughing fit brought a nurse to my side. She gave me a spoonful of some licorice-tasting syrup that killed my cough with sweetness.

I noticed I had blood caked around my cuticles and quicks, as well as mud, pink fibers, oil and other unmentionable substances. The thought of my father seeing my hands like that was too much for me. I slipped them under the covers and felt my face begin to quiver and my eyes fill with tears until I thought my eyelids would explode.

"Doesn't matter. You're fine. You're here." He made it sound as profound as it was.

"And where's Larry?" I asked.

"Don't worry, he'll be here."

"That wasn't what I was worried about."

"He's down with the police filling in the gaps."

"What gaps?"

"In the story, of how it happened."

"Daddy, I don't think Larry's story and mine are going to match–not perfectly."

"It'll all come out in the wash, Kory."

"Obviously, you have not done much laundry, Dad."

"I'll come do your laundry until you're feeling better," Mama volunteered, approaching the bed again.

A different nurse came in, and was filling a small pink plastic basin with warm water from the wash bowl tap.

"You think I could sleep within a mile of that cellar?"

"We'll talk about it later."

The nurse approached the bed and took my hands from beneath a sheet so clean I could feel the white against the skin of my forearms. She put my fingers in the warm water. I closed my eyes with the luxury of it.

"It's not a topic of discussion, Mama. Everything's different now."

My mother, the magician, can change topics without turning a hair, efficiently wiping an issue from her adversary's mind with one short sentence.

"You didn't even get any painting done," she reminded me.

"Regrettably, no," I agreed while the nurse used the pointy end of an orange stick to scrape gunk from under my nails.

"And that was the whole point of our taking care of your son, after all."

My mother can really drive home a point.

"That was the idea," I snapped.

Using a Q-tip, the nurse gently rubbed the dried crap away from my cuticles. Small crescents of everything bad I had been wallowing in lately floated on the water in the pretty pink basin.

"You'd think there would have been something you could do," Mama sniffed.

"I tried to paint," I said, but tears prevented further discussion.

The nurse smiled in commiseration with me, patted my fingertips dry with a fresh hand towel, lifted the basin of disgusting water off my lap and took it across the room where she poured it into the basin and washed it down.

"I'll come back," she mouthed, for my benefit only.

"You don't know what Larry is capable of. Did you know he destroyed some of my paintings because he found them embarrassing?" I asked my parents.

"Kory!" my mother reprimanded me. "Why would any civilized person want to imprison anyone who was not a danger to others?"

"Actually, I did feel like a prisoner of war."

"War against whom?"

"Against me."

"Why would anyone declare war on you?" my mother snorted.

"Why would anyone order every fellow American who happened to be genetically Japanese into a prison camp during WWII?"

"You can't be comparing the internment to what happened to you?" my father chuckled uncomfortably. "Why, you were too young even to know about it when it was happening."

"Apparently, no one knew it was happening. Just like no one knew I was locked in a cellar for nine days."

"No, I didn't know you were in the cellar, Kory. I swear."

Hark, the perpetrator has entered the room.

My mother bustled over to Larry, reassuring him in her knives-in-fog whisper:

"She's in shock, I think. Don't mind what she says. All about interment, the internment, World War II and who knows what all."

"I've told the police exactly what happened, Kory, but I'd like a chance to tell you too," said Larry. He actually approached my hospital bed, baseball cap in hand, Tom Sawyer penitent for having dipped Becky Thatcher's braids in his inkwell.

"We can stay if you want," offered my father, leaning backwards as if the open door was sucking him out of the room.

"I've faced a dark cellar," I said. "Not afraid to face him."

"Of course you're not afraid of your own husband," my mother scolded me.

"It's okay," I waved them away.

"We'll go see Bertie gets a good lunch and come back this afternoon," Mama said.

"I want to see Bertie," I wailed, needing to hug him.

"You have pneumonia, dear," my mother explained.

"Oh."

"Don't you wear our girl out now, son!" my father laughed as he pulled my mother out the door.

Larry sat in the chair beside the bed, then, not liking to speak up to me in my high hospital bed, he hopped back up again. Fiddled with things on the swiveling bedside tray. Checked out the IV.

"Giving you fluids, huh?"

I nodded just perceptibly.

"It was awful," he said, his brow creased with pain.

"Yes, it was."

"Realizing what I had accidentally put you through."

"Must have been terrible for you."

"Not as bad as what you went through though," he corrected himself.

"I'm really tired, Larry," I sighed. I did not want to hear his self-serving version of events at the moment—maybe ever.

"They said you slept straight through last night!"

"It'll take a while to catch up," I murmured.

"Not exactly a feather bed down cellar, huh?" he chuckled.

"Too soon for jokes I don't make, Larry," I said.

"But...," he stuttered, too confused to come up with a rejoinder. It was, after all, the first time I had not laughed at one of his jokes.

He wandered around the room, looking at objects that would not bear much close examination: the flat, featureless painting of a landscape in various unnatural shades of green; the shapeless gauzy curtains, the almost indecipherable doctor's notes on the clipboard. He spent a long minute contemplating the IV drip bag.

"What exactly are they putting into you?"

"I don't know. I just woke a while ago."

"I ought to ask the doctor."

"Why the sudden interest in what fluids I ingest?"

"I'm your husband. I'm supposed to keep an eye out for what doctors and so forth are doing to you."

"Nine days late," I muttered.

"Excuse me?" he flared, then reined in his anger. "I didn't come here to argue. I came to say how much I wish–it was a terrible thing that happened, and I want you to know it was just–as you said at the time, I got a little upset. That's how the mistake happened. You can see that. Nakamura had been pressing to use our land, and I knew what that was all about."

"Maybe it was just about his wanting to expand his farming business?"

"You don't know him, Kory! He's always been a lecher–eyeing every girl in school as they walked by our locker."

"That's what teenage boys do, as I recall– you included."

"He didn't want the land: He wanted you."

"And all the while I was wondering what you wanted."

Silence and the smell of antiseptic, and my husband shoving a piece of dust around on the floor with his shoe.

"Anyway," Larry prompted, "You spent nine days in a dark place, and you survived. I know it was horrible for you, but I'll bet it put that old fear of dark places to rest."

"It isn't the dark I dread. It's being constrained."

"I told you I never intended to shut you down cellar."

"From my point of view, intention is beside the point. The point is that thoughts of the internment plagued me while I was in the cellar. It was like suffering a national emergency inside me."

"Oh, please! All this talk about your being imprisoned in your own home is just you trying to impress Nakamura. 'Oh, Nicky!'" Larry cried, mincing around the room, doing his excellent imitation of me. "'Now I know just how you felt being interned by that nasty President Roosevelt. I am just an ordinary little white girl who–incidentally--owns her own farm with some excellent loamy bottom land. Poor me! I have been left out of the important events of my time. I sat at home with my *Life* books of World Wars I and II looking at pictures of starving orphaned children in war-torn lands and felt so sorry for them. Incidentally, I also felt sorry for myself because I never had a part in all that exciting action. I put no one in a concentration camp. I fought in no war. I was not myself interned. Locked myself in a closet once: surely that qualifies me for martyred sainthood. And now that I'm all grown up, I sit at home magnifying every tiny discomfort in my life so that I'll feel important. But, I'm just an unimportant little Caucasian chick trying to be important by claiming to have been imprisoned like the Japanese Americans, because I think a real family tragedy would bring me a little excitement."

My mouth fell open and I gasped in more air than I had breathed in nine days in the cellar. I was deciding whether to laugh out loud or to leap out of the bed and throttle Larry.

Just then Nick walked into the room.

"And here's Mr. Excitement now!" Larry cried, "My wife and I are having a private talk at the moment. You'll have to excuse us."

"Your private talk could be heard all the way to the nurse's station," said Nick. "Besides, since I was a featured object of your talk, I would really like to add my two cents worth."

"If I give you the two cents, will you just leave?" Larry took some change from his pants pocket and tossed it at Nick.

Nick picked two of the copper pennies off the floor and stuck them in his watch pocket.

"After I give you your money's worth."

"This visit is not appropriate." Larry muttered and sat on the end of my bed with his arms across his chest.

"We are neighbors, after all," Nick said. "I wouldn't want an oversight or two to come between us."

"Then you admit I'm not liable for the quicksand, and–the big internment my wife suffered?"

"I have no idea if you are legally liable," Nick said.

"I didn't know! About the cellar door, or anything."

"It fell shut with a sound like a clap of thunder. How could you have thought it was the door falling a few inches against a tree," I objected.

"And I knew nothing about the quicksand," Larry continued.

I gasped. "Daddy told me you knew about the quicksand and the whole liability thing, Larry."

Wheeling to face me, Larry stepped close to my hospital bed, as if to block my voice from reaching Nick.

"Learn some loyalty, Kory," he said, his eyes filling with tears. Leaning on the bed, he pulled the bedspread taut across my chest and I coughed.

Nick moved to the foot of the bed and looked at me with concern.

"You okay, Kory?"

"Excuse me," Larry said, "if I claim a brief intimate moment with my wife."

"I'm not here to cause any trouble," Nick apologized. "Between you two or between anyone and the law."

"The law." Larry jumped away from the bed as if it had spat at him. "As I have been explaining to Kory, what happened was a mistake. I have nothing to be ashamed of. I'm not a criminal."

"You're a little sloppy about closing cellar doors." I spoke in a clear voice for once. I did not even cough.

Larry jumped in surprise. "For all I know you shut the door on yourself."

"Because that's what people with claustrophobia do." I had to laugh.

"For all I know Nick did it. If he couldn't have you, no one could."

I stopped breathing for a moment and Nick and I gaped at Larry.

Nick squared his shoulders towards Larry. "For me it wasn't so much that you shut the door– I can never know whether or not that was an accident. What got me was your reaction when you found out about the cellar."

Imitating Nick, Larry squared his shoulders at him. "Really? What was that like for you?"

"Your first words were not, 'Are you okay, Kory?'"

"Blah-blah-blah. That was so much more than two cents worth. Ta-ta now!"

"In case you don't remember, Larry, you said, 'Who did this?' Looking for somebody to blame rather than for some way to comfort your wife."

Larry's eyes darted around the room as if he were looking for a better excuse written on the walls. "I was not surprised when you walked in the room." Larry sauntered to the table, which held a vase full of daisies some unknown sympathizer had brought me. He plucked a daisy and began playing a noisy game of She Loves Me Not with it.

Nick sighed impatiently. "I'm only here to see how Kory's doing and to renew my offer to farm the bottom land and the land the orchard stands on."

"You blackmailing me?" Larry scolded Nick by flapping the daisy mockingly at Nick.

Nick and I both looked at Larry.

"Where do you get that?" I sat up in bed.

"Come on. You can see what he's doing. If I let him farm that land, he won't sue about his boy trespassing and blundering into that wet sand."

"I'm a farmer. The land's aching to be farmed is all I'm saying."

"You think I'm going to believe that, after all the history between my family and yours?"

"There's no history between Kory's family and mine." Nick spoke low.

"So, you're not here to talk to me at all. You're here to talk to my wife, because you know her name is on the title. But who do you think maintains this land? Who will pay for the bulldozers and all that cement? Or maintain the drive that connects to River Road. How would you get your tractors down here without that? Who will pay for the man hours it took to get that bottom land clear?"

"Nick already told you he would do that."

"And I would."

"You two leave me nothing–no dignity, no place to stand," Larry shook his head, and looked from one of us to the other. "My family has been here longer than most families in this town have been on this continent. The land that your family lost to mine while you were in prison...."

"Interned," I corrected him.

"In whatever. It was just farm land to Nick. To the Stamps–to my family–it is the place where we stand. On principle. You get that?"

"Principle?" I asked, incensed. "The principle of unjustified possession?"

"Let's just talk about practicalities for a while." Nick spoke gently. "I'm a farmer. The old Nakamura farm is now the Stamp farm. It's gone, as far as we Nakamuras are concerned. A bit of American history. We'll never again try to get that back. But yours and Kory's land needs to be made healthy and productive again. I am only a farmer, and I would love to see that

190

land bloom again. Will you let me farm it? If we can make this deal, I think we will all have a place to stand together, as neighbors."

"Using the bad feelings between us and our families as bargaining chips is no place for anybody to stand," Larry argued.

"Where do you *get* that?" I felt my face flush with anger.

"Our land as payment for his grudge."

"Really, Larry, I'm just glad my kid is alive, and that Kory's okay."

Larry bent close to Nick with a smirk. "I guess you think she's more than okay, since you gave her a bath."

"No offence, Kory, but I did the same for my horse when she fell into a ditch and I found her covered in feces, dirt and bug bites," Nick snapped.

"You bathed my wife, asshole."

"I didn't bathe *with* her, for Christ's sake. Listen, maybe I'll come back to talk about leasing some land when time has healed those wounds." Nick nodded at us both, ran his hand through his hair, tipped his hat to me and headed for the door.

"Wait a minute, buddy." Larry grabbed Nick's shoulder and turned him around. "You can't just throw American history in my face and walk off like that. The Stamp farm is mine, not yours!"

Suffocating with impatience, I fell back on my pillow. "That's what he said, Larry."

"I'm going to go now." Nick made a move to pass Larry, but Larry planted himself in front of Nick. He balled up his fists and poked them into his thighs.

"No, you don't. I want you to admit that you are trying to get Stamp farmland to make up for land you claim we stole from the Nakamuras."

"Larry, he already told you...."

"This is between me and Nick, Kory."

"No, it isn't. The Stamps wrongly kept the Nakamura's farm they had been keeping for them during the internment, and they possess it wrongly to this day. When I found out about it, I felt sick and ashamed to belong to a race of people who would do such a thing. I'm part of American history too, Larry."

"You stay out of this, Kory."

With an effort, I resisted the urge to cough. "I have a legal right to be in it. I have the only right to be in on it, as far as this family and the old orchard land is concerned."

"You see how she is?" Larry seemed to collapse somewhere along the length of his spine. Breaking away from Nick, he scooped up the bouquet from its vase. Water and soggy leaves fell to the floor. "You deal with her. I give up. I brought her these flowers, you know, when she was lying in this bed gasping for air like a fish I had landed, and has she thanked me for them? Not that I recall. Now, I don't care anymore. I hope you two will be very happy together." With that he threw the sopping wet bouquet onto my chest, and offered this parting shot as he pulled open the door, "Oh, goody, the bride caught the bouquet!" He slammed the door shut behind him while smelly vase water drizzled down the neck of my hospital gown and Nick and I stared after him open mouthed.

I do not claim to have inherited my mother's famed ESP, but I was struck by the feeling that Larry did not want me anymore and had not for what seemed a long time. Observing his sudden mood change from adamant to devil-may-care, was like watching his possessive side give up a long struggle with his lack of passion for me. Even so, he could not stand to take the blame for ending our marriage.

"So, this unwelcome episode of my life begins and ends with Larry slamming a door in my face. Suddenly, I find that funny."

"Did you know he moved back in with his folks down river?" Nicky asked.

I was stunned.

"Said your place was too full of painful memories."

"Mine or his?" I breathed.

"Maybe both?"

"I'll have to get a job, rent an apartment, find a day school for Bertie–all those necessary things to find when your life changes overnight." I was muttering, twisting the soggy counterpane into spit balls with my fingers.

Nick leaned his hips against the bed and picked up the flowers.

"Want to keep these?" he asked, holding them over the waste basket.

"The only thing I want to keep from all this is Bertie."

"What about your house?"

"I'm going to have to relinquish that epoch of my life outright."

He dumped the flowers in the waste basket and put a stack of tissues under my chin to sop up the flower water. "The clientele at Skippy's General Store and Bait Shop on Main Street will be abuzz with the news."

"After emergency, fire, and police personnel strolled through the cellar and saw what a mess I made of the place, I'm way past caring what people think. I say let all the secrets in the world fly out of people's mouths the moment they happen, so people know what's going on around them and can plan their lives accordingly."

Nick gave me a wry look. "Not all that flies out of people's mouths is true."

"Oh! I'm sorry. If I sell my land, you can't rent it. And, here I am wanting my story to be blabbed all over the place, but your reputation has probably been afflicted too, what with Larry complaining at the top of his lungs that you bathed me and all."

"I stopped worrying about my reputation when I saw what carrying other people's shame did to my father."

"Other people's shame?"

193

"After the internment, my father was...altered. It's fortunate my brothers and I were still able to farm, because he wasn't. He went into the camp a strong-minded young father, and came out a few years later a befuddled old man."

"I'm sorry. I didn't know. About the internment, I mean--the appropriation of your family's land. I was as ignorant as a stump. I'm so ashamed of that. And of what my fellow white Americans and my white American president–my hero when I was a child–did to you."

He pulled off the sopping wet counterpane and sat on the bed next to my hip. "You didn't do it. And who was going to tell you? Internment 101 was not taught at school. No banner headlines in our papers and magazines. They didn't even talk about it down at Skippy's."

"I should have sensed something about the internment. You disappeared from right under my nose and I had no idea where you went."

"I'm sure you asked around–at least a little?"

"Not enough, apparently."

I fell back against my pillows.

"Kory, don't carry your government's shame the way my father did."

"The poor man. I always liked him. He kidded me mercilessly every time I was over at your house."

"His jolly ways evaporated after we were taken to the camp. And when we came back, his entire self was tied up in pretending it never happened."

"You never said. And yet you must have had a hard time of it too."

"I couldn't say anything to you about it. My father insisted none of us tell anyone where we had been. I can't say I didn't have--don't still have--some very dark thoughts about it. The ripple effect from Executive Order 9066 just keeps going and going. As we just saw, it still affects Larry's perception of us. But the way it affected my father.... Inside, I still carry his restriction against discussing that time."

Nicky paused for a moment to smooth the landscape of my bedding before looking up at me to plead for forbearance. Then he put his head down and plunged. I had seen the same look of determination against odds on his face when he was about to forego a pass play as Sacagawea High's star quarterback and run his compact body through a line of teenage behemoths for a game-winning touchdown.

He lowered his voice to a whisper, "Do you know, afterwards my father tried to farm, even though he was too confused to do it well? He would dress in his overalls and denim shirt every morning, put on his wool socks and work boots, slap on his old straw hat and go out into the fields every day. He pulled a few weeds, and also some of the seedlings. I hired a worker to go along behind him and replant the vegetables. My father would only try to work on the land closest to the road, because he wanted it to appear to others that he was still farming– as if we had never been away. That's what we said about the internment: *We were away.* When the tractor wasn't being used, I kept it locked in its shed for fear he would try to drive it and hurt himself. This way of life went on for years, through my marriage to Donna, the birth of Hank. But, one day one of my workers left the shed unlocked and the tractor key in the ignition. He stepped away for just a few minutes, and my father got the tractor started and drove it to the sloping field beside the road. Donna was down there taking lunch to the workers when the tractor came along the ridge. He drove it along a slope much steeper than those he had taught me to avoid. The tractor, unable to negotiate the pitch of a shoulder of land, fell over on Donna and threw my pop onto the side of the road. Donna was crushed by the tractor and my father died with a broken neck. I fired the worker who had left the tractor unprotected, but it was the internment that killed my father and my wife."

I needed to cough, but was too stunned even to breathe.

Nick sat bent over on my bed. "That's why I don't let what the gossips down at Skippy's say about me make me feel ashamed. The shame other people ought to feel can kill you."

I reached a hand up to his shoulder. "I have been having a fantasy lately about running away or digging a deep hole through the pump house floor all the way to the other side of the world. Bertie and I would pack our duffle bags and sneak away to a world where we could be ourselves. I suppose I was wishing I could run away from the shame I felt about my painful marriage. Now, I have to get a place of my own right away because the shock waves from one slammed door shook apart my family."

He chuckled softly. "I hope you won't run too far away. I'd miss you. Couldn't you move in with...?"

"My parents? They insist I need to work it out with Larry. Besides, my parents don't know where they leave off and I begin. I too had blurry boundaries at the time I was down cell...shut into the cellar. Living with my folks would be perilous to my health."

"I have an empty bunkhouse where you could stay. It's clean and cozy," he grinned. "Like the Three Bears' cottage in the woods."

"Then we really would be the talk of Salmon Run."

"I have room. We get along. Our boys are the same age. Simple."

"After my divorce is final, maybe." I had a small coughing fit. "Wow, did I say the words *my divorce*?"

"Why not, if you don't care what other people think?"

"I won't say I haven't had my fantasies."

"No comment." Nick actually blushed.

"I have to ask you something, Nick." I tried to look him in the eye. "Larry goes on and on about how you were interested in leasing my land only because you were interested in my...self."

Nick laughed. "I doubt if that's exactly the way he put it, but I have to admit I liked the thought of dabbling in your acreage. Don't get me wrong, that is the best farmland in the area for the kind of crops I want to grow, but I did think we might be friends again."

"Even though you knew Larry was suspicious of your motives?"

"Yeah...Larry. In high school, if he saw a pretty girl walking down the hall, he would always make a comment about her amenities to me."

"Her amenities?"

"That's what we called her figure and such. But, if I said anything about a girl, Larry would look hurt, as if I had taken away his favorite toy and dropped it in a mud puddle."

"And the idea of farming land owned by a member of the Stamp family–if only by marriage–that didn't bother you?"

"I won't say what happened between our families during the war hasn't made me uncomfortable over the years. It's as if a tick keeps biting you under your collar for a couple decades. I thought a Nakamura's profiting from planting on Stamp land would be some retribution anyway. Sorry, Kory, to have thought of your land that way. I was ashamed of the feeling, and thought if you and I became friends again, I could remain clear in my mind that I was not getting back at you. And, that there was no way I could ever get back what the real Stamps took from my family."

"You were uncomfortable with me?"

"You know we have always been more than comfortable together as people. Though, I must say that I was never that comfortable with the idea of you as Mrs. Stamp."

I nodded. "That makes two of us."

Laughing, we reached out and shook one another's hands.

"I can make no new bonds since Donna." He spoke in a voice so low I hung my head off the bed to hear it. "But I already have a bond with you."

While I thought about that, he absent-mindedly reached his fingers around inside my cupped hand.

"When Bertie and I are free...."

"He and Hank could play together every day," he said, trapping my pinkie finger against my palm with his thumb.

"When my divorce is final." I faltered, freeing my finger from his grasp.

"Every day, all day." Nick grinned, stalking my ring finger with his thumb.

"But I pay you a fair rent." I moved my fingers furiously to avoid capture.

"The fairy tale cottage is empty anyway, so there's no need." He trapped my ring finger.

"There's an old debt I need to pay off." That surprised him and I was able to free my ring finger and begin to stalk his index finger.

"You owe me nothing," he said. His fingers were faster and stronger than mine, just as they had been in primary school.

"Let's say it's a family debt." I tried to pin his finger. "My son's family. I intend to get custody in the divorce, but Bertie was born a Stamp. I don't want him to have any regrets when he is old enough to know about the internment and the Nakamura/Stamp farm. "

"I will charge you a dollar a year as long as you rent the cottage." Our hands struggled together, playing the old game.

"That's not nearly enough." I slipped my thumb past his index finger and used my nail to pin his pinkie against his palm.

"Ow!" he cried, pulling his hand away.

"Oh, sorry! But I win at last! I have to pay you a reasonable rent, right?"

He laughed, rubbing his pinkie finger. "Fine, if it means that much to you."

"I apologize for the fingernails. I don't bite them the way I did in grade school."

"I was just caught off guard."

"I know how that feels."

Nick held out his hand to me.

"Rematch?"

I reached my hand across the bed.

Outcomes

The days slipped by--days of doctors, clean stiff white sheets, pillows that smelled like heaven, intravenous injections of liquid to correct dehydration and anemia, antibiotics to squash the pneumonia, all wiped away by the happy reunion with my little boy after the doctors got the pneumonia under control. Bertie told me he had seen the "biggah bumblebee in the world," and that Gramma helped him make a little thimbleberry pie all for himself.

My mother would not come to get me from the hospital.

"That's your husband's place," she said.

"You think I should live with a man who shut me in the cellar?"

"I'm with your father on this one. If you're keeping count, that's about the third time in the history of the world."

I could not go back home. As far as I was concerned, my husband had proved himself a danger to me, though he had done it in such a way that his malicious intent could never be proven in a court of law. Before I could call Larry to tell him I wanted a divorce, he sent his lawyer to the hospital with divorce papers and a request for twice-a-month weekend visitation rights with our son. I had my lawyer tell his lawyer that I agreed to everything. Although I would always have an underlying fear of Larry's mysterious animosity towards me, I knew he loved Bertie so did not believe Larry was a threat to him.

Larry married again as soon as he was legally able, and I was grateful for her sake that–though she was an apprentice weather girl at the station where Larry worked– she gave it all up to be a housewife. Larry liked to have a wife who was always waiting for him at home and it was nice he would not have to imprison her in the cellar to get her to do it.

It has not been easy. What I did know was that I

would have to remind myself every hour of the day that I had a right to paint. Larry's voice pops into my head to this day, trying to whittle me down to size. But I recognize the voice now for what it is, the memory of things he has said to me. Not a part of me. Just part of my memory of him.

The family property is completely different now than it was when I was growing up. I sold it to a couple who made it into a family park. There are picnic tables, swings, a water slide into a deep pool on "my" side of the river, and a self-propelled merry-go-round. The residence doubles as a restaurant and snack stand. But the real attraction is Devil's End, the quicksand pots which are separated from thrill seekers by an unattractive (I am told) cyclone fence. The biggest day for Salmon Run on Halloween is the Gates of Hell attraction where thrill seekers are taken by candlelight through a colorful flame-painted gate in the cyclone fence. There they watch in synthesized horror as an apparently terrified crash dummy propelled by an invisible rod and wearing a devil's outfit is chased into the pit through our creepy old orchard. On Halloween I can hear the raucous cheers, screams and applause during the excruciatingly slow descent of the devil doll into the quicksand.

My father and mother reported this grotesque ceremony to me, bemoaning what I had allowed to happen to the family homestead. They have not complained much, though, since I reminded them of the danger on the land that they never warned me about in all the years I lived there. The present owners decided to capitalize on the quicksand and publicize it at the same time to prevent further accidents. I myself have not seen the property once since I sold it, but decades' worth of paintings of the view from my front porch are waiting in my memory to be added to my *Women of Myth*.

As for Nick and me, anyone down at Skippy's can tell you about that. I will tell you that Hank and Bertie share a nanny four hours a day while I paint and Nick farms, and our two shy boys are becoming wonderfully boisterous in one another's company. And Nick gave me the best gift in the world for my birthday. He hired Jimmy year-round to work on the farm and had him build some shallow wardrobes, drawers and shelves all along one wall of my room. Jimmy never has to sleep under an overpass and I never have to walk into a closet again.

The gallery owner generously moved the date of my gallery showing many months forward to give me time to digest the earth-change that occurred to me in the cellar. Now that this written narrative of my "internment" is complete, I sit on my painting stool, looking at a blank canvas like the one I put on my easel last August in anticipation of nine days of undisturbed painting. To heal from my adventure underground, I had attempted at first to paint the picture of the Hellenic maiden Danae I had mind-painted in the cellar. My brush had another plan, however, and I watched as a newly conceived painting of the true Danae, the universal goddess who had once graced the world before the revisionist patriarchs mangled her myth. In my new painting, the goddess Dana opens the sunroof of the princess Danae's prison and flies her out of her cellar on airy filigree wings of bronze--because goddesses can do that. She was Nick's ancestral deity, Amaterasu, the sun goddess, hiding from her brother, the storm god, in a cave, and then drawn out by her own image. She was also a small Native American girl rising out of quicksand. But, really, she was me, my own internal image, though Larry would not have thought so. Too fanciful for him, for sure, but, when it was done, I felt myself lifting on secret wings out of the confining self-image that had been other people's gift to me.

Now I paint in this airy studio on the Nakamura farm high atop the bluff where the dawn light behind Mt. Hood sparks my day. I can hear the Silky far below as my hand moves towards the easel to retrace the first brush stroke of *The Silver Thaw,* the painting once condemned to the fire by my husband, but conceived anew in the dark and ready to flow onto real canvas in this sun-bright room.

Bibliography

Edmonds, Margot and Clark, Ella E. "The Warm Wind Brothers vs. The Cold Wind Brothers." <u>Voices of the Winds: Native American Legends</u>. Castle Books, 2003.

Kennedy, Malcolm D. <u>A Short History of Japan</u>. The New American Library, Inc., 1964.

www.ingramcontent.com/pod-product-compliance
Lightning Source LLC
Chambersburg PA
CBHW070838120626
46556CB00002B/788